Also by Steve Hagood
From Indigo Sea Press

Chasing the Woodstock Baby

indigoseapress.com

Cold, Dark Places

By

Steve Hagood

Stiletto Books
Published by Indigo Sea Press
Winston-Salem

Stiletto Books
Indigo Sea Press
PO Box 67201
Winston-Salem, NC 27114
This book is a work of fiction. Names, characters,
locations and events are either a product of the author's
imagination, fictitious or used fictitiously. Any resemblance
to any event, locale or person, living or dead, is purely
coincidental.

For information regarding bulk purchases of this book,
digital purchase and special discounts, please contact the publisher
at indigoseapress@gmail.com

Cover design by Pan Morelli
Manufactured in the United States of America
ISBN 978-1-63066-469-5

In Cold Dark Places
I Dream of Spring

KD Lang.

Chapter One

April in The D. It's that special time of year when Detroiters wash the salt and winter grime off their cars, the hookers premiere the latest in spandex and the dead bodies left to rot in abandoned lots thaw out and start to stink.

That's how April's supposed to go. It's supposed to be spring, but Mother Nature seemed to have her calendar screwed up. It was colder than hell. Detroit had just endured the coldest and snowiest winter in its 314-year history, and it wouldn't go away. The Tigers game had been snowed out the night before. Other than the start of baseball season, Chase didn't much care for spring.

He sat at the bar in the pub he owned with Sarge. He drank coffee and wondered if that night's game would be played and whether or not to turn up the heat. The last cop pulled on his coat and exited with a wave. There'd be another group of them at the next shift change, but at that moment Sarge and Chase were alone in O'Ryan's.

Nicholas O'Ryan's great-great grandparents had emigrated from Ireland during the potato famine. He was as American as the next guy, but he built a good old-fashioned Irish pub that would have made his ancestors proud. The walls were covered with dark green wallpaper, the bar was mahogany with a brass foot rail and the lights were dim. His only mistake had been building it pretty much right across the street from police headquarters. The cops had adopted the place as their own, and it had been the local cop bar ever since. Nicholas hadn't intended for it to be the local cop bar, but business was good so he adapted.

"Hey, Chase," Sarge said from behind the bar where he worked on a crossword puzzle. "Help me out here. Six letters. The clue is 'Oscar winner Washington.'"

1

"Bite me, old man," Chase said to his former training officer.

Ever since Trudy DeRosa's article about Chase's finding the Woodstock Baby had gone viral, his phone had "blown up," as the kids say. People he had never met wanted him to find everything from their long-lost relatives to their car keys. Chase had also been approached by some people from Hollywood who wanted to make a movie about the investigation. They had promised to get Denzel Washington to play him, even though Chase was white, younger than and nowhere near as pretty as Denzel. He had turned them down, but it didn't stop his former colleagues from the Detroit police force from calling him Denzel whenever they got the chance.

Sarge laughed and went back to his puzzle. Chase went back to wondering about the game.

The door to the street opened. The man who entered wore a shiny, black, satin jacket that said "Joe Louis Basketball" on the left chest, black warm-up pants and a pair of Air Jordan basketball shoes. He stood six-seven and looked like he could still run the wing for Detroit State University, if you overlooked the limp. Twenty years earlier he had taken a nasty fall during a first-round NCAA tournament game. His leg had shattered and ended his career, along with the Thunderbirds' best chance at a national title.

"Hey, Ty," Chase said.

Ty Jackson smiled and limped to the bar. His skin was a paler shade of black than his coat, but not much. His teeth gleamed in the dimness of the bar. Ty was the head basketball coach at Joe Louis High School. He and Chase had become friends while working with the Detroit Police Athletic League. In the under-the-table recruiting world that was high school basketball in the city, Ty's rivals claimed he worked with the PAL to get an *in* with the kids while they were young. Chase knew better. He knew how much Ty

2

loved the game and enjoyed teaching it.

"What brings you down here?" Chase said when Ty had settled on the stool next to his.

"Just like that?" Ty said. "No 'how do you do?' No offer of a drink?"

"I'm sorry, Ty. It's just that everybody is after me for something these days. How do you do? Care for a drink?"

Ty nodded in satisfaction. "Coffee would be great. It's colder than shit out there."

"That it is," Chase said. He moved behind the bar to retrieve the coffee. He placed a steaming mug in front of Ty and then leaned his forearms flat on the bar.

Ty took a small sip and returned the mug to the bar. "You hear about the girl who went missing from D State? Apparently, they had been at a party with a bunch of basketball players. It was the night the team won their conference tournament and qualified for the big dance."

"And?"

"There's a rumor going around that she was last seen with Bowe Bradlee. I hear the police have started to take an interest in him."

"Bowe was one of your players," Chase said…. as if Ty didn't know.

Ty nodded.

"Have you talked to him?"

"No. He sent me a text that said, 'I didn't do it' and I haven't heard from him since. He's missing now as well."

"Missing? Or hiding?"

Ty nodded and sipped again from his coffee. "Probably hiding," he conceded. "He's just a kid, Chase. He's scared. Where he grew up, things like this don't go well for people like him."

Chase didn't say anything. He refilled his coffee cup from the pot.

"He's a good kid, Chase."

3

"Why you telling me?"

"I need your help. This kid has a chance to make it out of this place. Hell, they're saying he's probably gonna go first in the draft."

Chase sighed. "Shit, Ty."

"I need to know where Bowe is or at least that he's safe."

After his father and Sarge, Ty Jackson was the most forthright and decent man Chase had ever known. "I'm not supposed to get involved in police business. I could lose my pension, not to mention my license."

Sarge snorted a laugh. "When has that ever stopped you?"

"Shut up, old man," Chase said. But Sarge was right. Chase had never been one to follow orders. It was why he had been forced out of the DPD before he had been ready. Which was why, despite the fact that he really didn't need the money—he had his pension from the force and his stake in O'Ryan's—he had obtained a private investigator's license. The action was what he needed.

"They made me sign a non-compete when they gave me the retirement."

"Get outta here," Ty said incredulously.

Chase held up his hand like a witness swearing to tell the truth, the whole truth and nothing but the truth. "I swear."

"I've never heard of such a thing."

"What can I say? It's Detroit."

Chase took a deep breath and studied his old friend. Ty's eyes pled with him.

"What's the deal with you and this kid?" he said.

Ty shrugged, trying for nonchalant. "He's one of my kids."

"Come on, Ty. Spill it."

Ty sighed. "Bowe comes from the street, Chase. He's never known his father, and his mom's an addict. She's homeless. He was living with his grandma, but she died.

Wanda and I took him in. Wanda loves him like her own. He's the child we've never had."

"Does she know what's going on?"

Ty grimaced and rubbed the back of his head.

Chase laughed. He wouldn't have wanted to be the one to tell her either. "Okay," he said. "I'll ask around and see if I can figure out what's going on."

Ty grinned. "Thanks, man."

"But no promises."

Chapter 2

Homicide was housed in the new Public Safety Headquarters. The seven-story gray and green office building, renovated from the MGM casino after they moved into their fancy new digs, had replaced the ages-old, grime-covered block of limestone that had housed police headquarters for more than eighty years. Chase parked and took it in. It was nice, but he missed the old dump at 1300 Beaubien.

He entered into a quiet lobby that reminded him of a doctor's office. This was where the brass worked. It wasn't where the criminals were. They were at the precincts spread around the city. He told the guy behind the counter he was there to see Commander Maurice Warrick. The guy didn't speak; he just pointed to the waiting area. So Chase sat and waited.

He and Warrick had gone to the academy together. Warrick had fast-tracked from there while Chase had done the one-step-forward, two-steps-back thing until he had two-stepped his way right the hell out of the department.

Warrick appeared through the glass door behind the reception counter. He was black with a short afro sprinkled with gray. He wore the dark-blue DPD uniform. The badge on his chest shone almost as much as his shoes.

A faint *buzz* and *clunk* preceded the door opening. Warrick pulled the door open and crooked a finger, summoning Chase. They took the stairs; Chase wondered why. Did Mo not want to be seen with him?

They exited the stairwell on the third floor and walked down a short corridor to an office. Warrick settled behind an Office Max desk while Chase took in the view of the Lodge Freeway out the window.

"Nice place ya got here, Mo," he said.

"Yeah, but I kinda miss 1300," Warrick said, speaking for the first time. His voice was soft and modulated. It didn't match the six-foot-two, powerfully-built man who had worked his way up the chain of command in the police department of the most dangerous city in America; but it was Warrick's voice, and it commanded respect which the rank and file gave without hesitation.

Chase smiled and sat in one of the chairs facing the desk.

"You just come to check out my new office?"

"That okay?"

Warrick smiled. "Sure, I'm always up for a visit from an old comrade who washed out."

"Retired," Chase said.

Warrick chuckled. "What do you want, Chase?"

"Why'd we take the stairs?"

"I love you and all, but you aren't exactly the most popular person around here. In fact, if the chief knew you were here, he'd throw your ass out himself."

"What'd I do?"

"You stirred the pot with the city council. We don't have to like 'em, but we have to work with 'em. They hold the purse strings."

Chase frowned. "The kid did it, Mo."

"But his mama is a big shot on the council."

"So I was supposed to give him a walk?"

Warrick smiled the smile that one gives the dumb kid. "This your first day in Detroit?"

"He was guilty."

"He was," Warrick conceded with a nod. "And that's the *only* reason you got a pension. Don't give them a reason to take it away."

Chase decided to change the subject. "What's the scoop on the missing girl from D State?"

Warrick shook his head. "Did you not hear what I just said?"

7

"I got a visit from Ty Jackson," Chase said. "He's concerned about his boy Bowe. I told him I'd ask a couple of questions. See what I could find out."

"Uh-huh," Warrick said, poker face firmly ensconced.

"Come on, Mo. Help a brother out."

Warrick chuckled, shaking his head. "You're the palest brother I ever did see. Regardless, I don't have a scoop to give you. I don't know anything about it."

"So there's no case ongoing?"

"Hold on." He picked up the phone on the desk and dialed. He asked whoever answered about the missing girl and then hung up. "A file has been opened," he said with a shit-eating grin. "But I doubt there has been much investigating."

"Who has the file?"

"Sergeant Clinton."

"Aw shit," Chase said.

Warrick laughed. "You still fuckin' his wife?"

"Ex-wife. And they were separated at the time."

"I don't think ol' Andy saw the distinction."

Chase winced. He knew ol' Andy hadn't seen the distinction. Clinton had been convinced that Chase was the reason his marriage had ended. He remembered quite clearly the night Clinton had threatened to shoot him and probably would have if he hadn't been too drunk to find his gun.

"Was the sex worth it?" Warrick asked.

"Oh hell, yes," Chase said.

Warrick laughed so hard he almost fell out of his chair. Chase laughed too but wasn't looking forward to dealing with ol' Andy.

Andy Clinton sat with his feet on the desk, ankles crossed, fingers laced behind his head and his eyes closed. The casual observer might think he was sleeping, but he wasn't asleep; he just didn't give a shit. He had been a good

8

cop once—young, eager and idealistic. He had thought that he could make a difference. He had grown up with great admiration for police officers. They had been the line in the sand that had divided the good from the bad. They had protected Andy and his family and friends from the people who would bring them harm. Andy had joined the police cadets in high school. He got a tee-shirt and a whistle and helped work crowd-control at parades and fairs. Yes, it had been hokey and some of the cool kids had teased him, but screw them. He was making a difference in his community and making something of himself while those losers were smoking dope and whatever else those losers did when they didn't invite him.

He joined the Detroit Police even though his parents had moved out of the city, along with almost all of the other white people, following the '67 riots. It wasn't until he was a few years in that he realized just how bad it was. The city was rampant with crime and corruption, and that was the government! Mayor Coleman A. Young the Crook was the first to have his hands in the till. Forty years later, the "Hip Hop Mayor" Kwame Kilpatrick was sentenced to twenty years; but it had taken the feds to do it as Kwame bragged he could still get elected if he could get his name on the ballot. Clinton scoffed at the whole thing. The blacks rioted because they wanted to control the city and look what they did with it. From being named the murder capital of the world to becoming the first major city in history to declare bankruptcy, Detroit was deservedly the butt of every joke.

Clinton had cared for a while and tried to do his best. It was about the time that his wife left him that he gave up. He had just less than three years until his pension vested, and then he was out of there. He was going to cash in and head North. Until then, he didn't plan on moving his ass from that chair.

The detective bureau was cut into a rat maze by chest-high walls covered in bluish-gray fabric. Andy Clinton sat in his assigned cube with his feet on the desk. Was he asleep? Chase took the offensive, shoving Clinton's feet from the desk. The rocked-back chair sprang forward, almost catapulting his worthless ass.

"Rise and shine, jackass," Chase said.

It took a moment for Clinton to determine what had happened. When he did, he came out of the chair with clenched fists.

Warrick appeared, resting his forearms on the top of Clinton's cubicle wall. "I was just telling Chase what a great job you're doing on the Aley Beach case, Sergeant Clinton," he said.

Clinton retreated a step, but held his glare on Chase. "What case is that, Commander?"

"Aley Beach," Chase said, "the girl missing from D State."

"Oh, right," Clinton said. Not a trace of embarrassment showed from forgetting the girl's name, which amazed Chase.

"So what have you got?"

"About what?"

"The missing girl," Chase said. "You have investigated something other than the insides of your eyelids, haven't you?"

"Not much to investigate," Clinton said. "The roommate filed a report after she said she hadn't heard from her in a couple of days. The parents confirmed that they hadn't heard from the girl either. I'm awaiting further developments."

"That's it?"

"Oh, and the roommate said that the girl's suitcase was missing, along with some of her clothes."

"Some?" Chase said. "Like maybe she went somewhere for a few days?"

"Right." Clinton smiled as if his theory had been confirmed.

"And you figure she'll turn up, and you won't have to get off your ass and look for her?"

"Hey, fuck you, Chase!" Clinton said, the smile gone. "A nineteen-year-old packs a bag and leaves for a few days. What am I supposed to do?"

"It's been more than a few days, dumb-ass."

Clinton shrugged. The worthless prick actually shrugged his fucking shoulders.

"Like I said, I'm awaiting developments."

Chase snorted and shook his head at the incompetence. "What's this rumor I hear about Bowe Bradlee?"

"Who?"

"The basketball player."

"Oh, right, Mr. Superstar," Clinton said, doing nothing to hide his disdain. "The roommate said she had seen the girl, Abby—"

"Aley."

"—last in the presence of the basketball player. I talked to him and he denied it."

"And?"

"And what?" Clinton said. "I'm awaiting further developments."

"Like I said," Warrick laughed.

"Yep," Chase said, "doing a fine job."

They started to walk away, but Clinton called Chase back. He stepped into Chase's personal space and quietly said, "Now that I know you have an interest in this case, I'm gonna squash that nigger like a bug."

"Is that right?"

"That's right."

Chase shook his head. He seemed to do a lot of that around Andy Clinton. "You know," he said, "it's possible the kid didn't do it."

11

"Well," Clinton said, grinning like a jack-o-lantern, "that don't really matter now, does it?"

Chase turned to leave, but Clinton called him back again. He pulled open his suit coat with his left hand. A nine-millimeter automatic hung in a shoulder rig. "I know where my gun is now."

Chapter 3

Sally sat at the bar, working on her laptop when Chase returned to O'Ryan's. She wore blue jeans and a gray Henley shirt with the top two buttons undone and the sleeves pushed up to her elbows. Her strawberry-blonde hair was pulled into a ponytail, and she wore just a dusting of makeup. Seasoned detective that he was, Chase could never figure out what it was that Sally did that took so long in the morning. How long does it take to pull your hair into a ponytail? But whatever it was, it was worth it. She looked spectacular, as always. He watched her until she sensed his presence and looked up. She smiled and Chase's toes tingled.

"Hey, Chase," she said. "What's the haps?"

Sarge claimed that Sally was his niece, but Chase had his doubts. There was just no way this lovely creature was related to Sarge and his Easter Island head. Niece or not, she was the third wheel in the partnership. Actually, she was the big wheel that kept O'Ryan's moving forward. Before she had come along, Sarge and Chase had been driving the place into the ground. Apparently, fifteen years in law enforcement did not teach one to run a bar. Who knew?

Chase slid onto the stool around the bend of the bar from her and said, "Do you know how Lance Parrish got the nickname 'The Bigwheel'?"

"Who's Lance Parrish?"

Chase gasped and grabbed his chest. "Who's Lance Parrish?"

Sally nodded. "Yes. Who's Lance Parrish?"

"Only the catcher of the best damn baseball team ever to wear the old English D."

"Oh," Sally said, "the vaunted '84 Tigers."

"Damn right the '84 Tigers!"

13

Sally laughed at Chase's indignation. "Okay, tell me. How did Lance Parrish get the nickname The Bigwheel?"

"Well…" Chase said, and then he saw the smirk on her lips and the twinkle in her eyes. He stopped. "You don't care, do you? You're just messing with me."

Sally laughed. "Sorry . What else is going on?"

Chase transitioned, trying not to show the hurt from her teasing. "Ty Jackson came to see me this morning."

"Who's that?"

"The varsity basketball coach over at Joe Louis High. He and I were friends back when I worked with the PAL."

"Oh," Sally said. "Well, that's nice."

"Not really."

"Why not?"

Chase told her about the disappearances of Aley Beach and Bowe Bradlee.

Sally listened intently and then said, "You should stay out of it. Let the police handle it."

"Yeah, well, I didn't tell you everything. I went over to police headquarters to ask around and see what was up with it all."

"Why don't I like the sound of that?"

Chase told her about his conversation with Clinton and the threats that Clinton had made.

"I feel responsible now. I can't let him hang this on Bowe."

"He threatened to shoot you?"

"Not in so many words. But that's not what's bothering me. Like I said, I don't want him to railroad this kid if the kid didn't do it."

Sally tapped on the laptop's keyboard. In another life she had been a paralegal, and her specialty had been research. She could pull information from the internet like nobody's business. Her help had been invaluable to Chase during the Woodstock Baby investigation. She stopped the assault on the keyboard and turned the laptop so Chase could see the screen. "Is that her?"

Chase looked at the screen. A girl's Facebook profile picture smiled out at him. Her blonde hair was streaked with pink. She looked drunk with glassy eyes and red cheeks. "I don't know."

"How many Aley Beaches can there be at Detroit State?"

"Good point." Chase scrolled through the pictures on the girl's page. In almost every one she looked drunk or high and was posed in ways that drunks think are funny: flashing the peace sign, giving the finger, dancing on the bar and falling off the bar among them. He turned the laptop back to Sally.

"She hasn't posted anything since the night she went missing," Sally said.

"That's probably not a good sign."

Sally agreed. "So what's the plan?"

"I don't know," Chase admitted. "My gut tells me that Bowe is okay. I think he's just hiding and awaiting further developments, along with Clinton."

"And the girl?"

"Yeah, the girl." Chase scratched the back of his head. "I'm not so sure about her. Everybody says she's an adult, and she can disappear if she wants to. But how many nineteen-year-olds disappear without telling someone?"

"Or posting something on Facebook or Twitter or Instagram or—"

"Right."

"You need to find the girl, Chase."

Chase nodded. "I'm on it, but I could use some of your special talent."

Sally smiled and tilted her head a little. "What talent are you interested in? I have a few."

Chase pointed at her computer. "See if you can find out where Bowe might be hiding. Does he have family in the area where he could be staying? His parents are out of the picture, but what about siblings? Or grandparents?"

Sally deflated. "Sure."

Chase noticed the deflation but had no idea what it was about. He had his hand on the door handle before it hit him. He turned back. "Were you—"

Sally shook her head. "Forget it, Chase. Just go."

Bowe Bradlee was definitely all right. At that moment he was popping the last piece of a New York strip in his mouth. He chewed slowly, savoring the taste of the top-grade beef. As a kid, he hadn't even known that something like steak and eggs existed. He had been happy if he had gotten a piece of toast for breakfast. But steak? For breakfast? Shit. He had never even seen a steak until Coach Jackson and his wife had taken him in prior to his junior year at Joe Louis, and even *they* didn't eat steak for breakfast.

He wheeled the room-service cart into the hallway and then turned around and took in his surroundings. He was in a suite in Birmingham in the hotel that Howard said the visiting NBA teams stayed at when they played the Pistons. It had a living room with a couch, two chairs, a big-screen TV and a fireplace. Through a door was a bedroom with a king-sized bed that even he fit on, another big-screen TV and a bathroom with a shower big enough to hold him and he didn't even have to bend over to wash his hair. For a kid from the streets of Detroit, this place was like the land of OZ.

Bowe laughed to himself and shook his head, all this because he was tall and could hoop.

The truth was, he had been scared when that white cop had come around asking about some girl at school. Had he been with the girl at a party? Really? Shit. Probably. But he didn't remember. He couldn't keep track of all of them college girls. But it did scare him. The white cop was racist. Bowe had been around enough crackers to be able to tell just by the way they looked at him and spoke to him. Some of them tried to cover it up, but he could always tell. That white cop, though, he didn't even try to cover it up. So Bowe had called Howard. Howard would fix it. Just like he had done with that crazy bitch who had said Bowe had raped her. Rape? Shit. He didn't rape no one. Didn't have too. They lined up to fuck Bowe.

The bedroom door opened, and a white woman entered the living area. She was older than Bowe was used to. She wasn't no college girl, that was for sure. She was a full-fledged woman Bowe had ordered off the internet, just like room service. Her titties were heavier than the college girls he was used to and hung a little lower, and her ass was a little wider; but she had done things to him that those college girls didn't even know about. He smiled at the memory and felt a stirring in his pants.

He couldn't remember her name, so he went with his go-to, "Hey, baby."

The lady smiled at Bowe. It wasn't an I-like-you smile; it was an I'm-being-nice-because-I-want-to-sell-you-something smile, like a saleswoman at Puffer Red's, the store where his grandma took him shoe shopping before she died. Bowe didn't care, though; he wanted to buy what she was selling.

"How about we have another go before you leave?"

The hooker was collecting up her things and sliding into her shoes. "Sorry, darling. You used up all your money last night."

"There's plenty more where that came from."

She looked at the growing bulge in Bowe's pants and shook her head. "No way. You keep that thing away from me."

Bowe laughed. "Too big for ya, huh? You white girls ain't used to takin' the anaconda."

17

Chapter 4

The Beaches lived in a farming community named Emerson, northwest of the city. It was about an hour's drive up I-75, then down three or four state routes, county roads and dirt roads. Chase finally came to a farm with a sign in the front yard that declared it a "Centennial Farm." He took that to mean that it had been there at least a hundred years.

The house was a two-story with white clapboard, like something Norman Rockwell had painted. An old, red two-story barn sat on the other side of the driveway. Further behind the red barn were metal structures, housing tractors and other farming equipment. Chase didn't have a clue what any of it did.

He bounced up a rutted, muddy driveway and parked next to a twenty-year-old pickup truck covered in mud and Confederate flag stickers. A slightly newer Ford Explorer, also covered in mud but without stickers, was parked on the other side.

The side door to the house slammed opened, and a middle-aged woman stood staring at him. She had dark hair cut short and no makeup. She looked as if she hadn't slept in days. She wore jeans, a flannel shirt over a gray tee-shirt and rubber boots up to her knees.

"Did you find her?"

"Are you Mrs. Beach?"

The woman shrieked. "Just tell me!"

She thought he was the police. He had purchased the black Charger he drove from a Wayne County Sheriff's department auction. It'd been stripped of the decals but still looked like a cop car.

"No."

Mrs. Beach had been drawn as tight as a guitar string

while awaiting the answer. She exhaled and wilted. "Damn."

Chase still hadn't even closed the car door. He did so. "My name is Chase. I wonder if I could ask you some questions."

"I don't know what we can tell you that we didn't tell the other detective but sure, come on in."

She held the wooden screen door open, the little spring at the top stretched to its fullest. Chase stepped through and into a big kitchen with a big butcher-block table right in the middle. It was warm and cozy. Chase imagined it was the perfect place to return to after a hard day working outside in the cold.

"Have a seat," Mrs. Beach said. "My husband will be in in a few minutes. I was just about to start dinner. Would you like some coffee?"

"Sure, if it wouldn't be too much trouble."

"Not at all. I was just about to put on a pot for John."

She pulled filters and coffee from the cabinets and filled the coffeemaker with water. She turned it on and then sat at the table.

"So you haven't found her yet?"

Chase shook his head. "No, ma'am."

"John and I are worried sick. She's never done anything this before."

"Anything like what?"

"Well, just up and took off. She's never really gone anywhere on her own."

"So you know about her suitcase then?"

"Yes."

"And you think she left of her own volition?"

"That's about the only thing that is keeping me from completely losing my mind. She *has* to just be off somewhere."

"But you filed a missing-persons report?"

"Well, yes," she said. "She hadn't told anybody where

she is, her phone is going straight to voice mail and she hasn't posted anything on Facebook, Twitter or Instagram."

The kitchen door opened, and a big bear of a man came in. "Whose car is that out there?" he said, shucking off rubber boots like the kind Mrs. Beach wore. Chase stood as the man hung a tattered, canvas coat on a hook above the boots.

"This is Detective Chase, John. He's new on Aley's case."

"What happened to that other guy, Clinton?"

"He's still on it," Chase said. "I'm just helping out. You know, like a fresh pair of eyes." It wasn't a complete lie. He intended to bring Clinton into the loop when he found something out. That's sort of like helping out.

Beach eyed Chase skeptically and then shook his head. "Whatever. Have you found her?"

"Not yet. I was hoping to ask you some questions and maybe get a look at her bedroom."

"Her bedroom? What's her bedroom got to do with anything?"

"I don't know. Maybe there's a clue in there somewhere."

"The other detective didn't want to see her room. Hell, he didn't even come out here."

No surprise there. "I'd still like to see it, if you don't mind."

Beach eyed Chase again and then shook his head. "Fine. Let's go."

He led Chase up a narrow staircase to the second floor. There were two small bedrooms to the right of the landing and one to the left with a bathroom in the middle. Beach turned right and into the bedroom on the right. At six-foot and 200 pounds, Chase was above average size. Beach was bigger than him, a lot bigger. Together they filled the small bedroom.

The walls were the color of the oceans on a world map. A flower-patterned area rug lay centered on the floor, covering one-hundred-year-old hardwood floors. There was a single bed with a white headboard decorated with small red roses and a short, wide dresser that was also white with roses. A mirror, lined with pictures wedged between the glass and the frame, was attached to the dresser. All but one of the photos were candid shots of teenagers acting like teenagers. The one that wasn't candid was a "formal" prom photo. Chase pointed at it. "Is that Aley?" She didn't look like the girl from Facebook.

Beach looked at the photo for a minute. Chase didn't think he was trying to discern if it were his daughter; he was admiring it.

"Yes."

"Who's the guy? Boyfriend?"

"Yes. His name is Dan Gentry. Aley and he have been dating for a few years."

"Do you know where I can find him?"

Beach chuckled. "I sure do. He works here on the farm for me." He looked out the window and pointed at the old beater truck. "That's his truck right down there."

"If you don't mind my saying, Aley doesn't look much like this anymore."

Beach sighed and sat on the bed. The springs groaned in protest. "She came home for Christmas with the piercings and streaks in her hair. The wife says it's a phase, and she'll grow out of it."

"What do you think?"

"I think we never should have let her go off to Detroit. I mean, *Detroit*. What the hell were we thinking? And now she's gone missing."

Chase nodded. He didn't know what to say to that. "Is it okay if I look around a little?"

Beach stood as if deadlifting the weight of the world and walked to the door. "Sure."

He went downstairs to check on the coffee and left Chase alone in his daughter's room. It wasn't the first time he had been in a teenage girl's bedroom, but he still felt like a creeper. But creeper or not, he went through her things. He checked in drawers and under drawers, between the mattresses and on the top shelf of the closet, everywhere a clue might be hidden. He didn't find one. Somewhere along the way an ungodly roar sounded. Chase looked out the window and saw the beater truck leaving.

When he turned back to the room, a dog lay on the bed. It was a black lab going gray around the muzzle. It looked at Chase with the same pleading eyes that Mrs. Beach had looked at him with.

Chase reached down and scratched the dog behind the ears. "I know. We'll find her."

He returned to the kitchen. John Beach sat at the table, staring into his coffee cup. His wife stood by the window looking at a swing set in the backyard. Chase wondered what she saw. Did she see the lonely, white, metal a-frame swing set with the slide covered in surface rust? More than likely she saw it as it looked the day her husband had set it up for their only child. The girl they had sent off to college had changed more than the swing set in the backyard, but neither were the same.

Neither of the Beaches had heard Chase enter. Both were lost in their individual thoughts. Chase cleared his throat. "You mind if I sit for a minute?"

Beach looked up and nodded at the chair. Chase pulled it out and sat. Mrs. Beach asked if he still wanted coffee. He declined.

"I know this is hard," Chase said. "I don't have children so I can't imagine what you're going through right now."

Beach nodded but didn't speak.

"I understand that neither of you has heard from Aley since the night her roommate last saw her. Is there anybody else she might have been in contact with during that time? Friends?"

"I can give you a list of her friends," Mrs. Beach said. She moved to the kitchen counter and pulled a notepad and a pen from a drawer.

Her husband shook his head. "She's not the same," he said in a low rumble. "We shouldn't have let her go."

There would be a time for shoulda, woulda and coulda. This wasn't it, but Chase wasn't going to tell him that. "It happens," he said. "Kids go off to college and make new friends and try new things." Drugs and sex were foremost in his mind, but how do you say that to a parent who's already freaked out? "New clothes, new hair... "

Mrs. Beach tore the top sheet off the notepad and handed it to Chase. "Here are a few names."

"The McAllister girl," John Beach said.

Chase scanned the list. "There's no McAllister on here."

"Her name is Meghan," Mrs. Beach said. "They aren't really close."

"She goes to the same school," Beach said. "They ride together sometimes when they come home. She's the only one I know who would know the old Aley and the new one."

The hurt radiating off the man when he said "the new one" was crushing. Damn kids. They had no idea what they put their parents through. "Okay," Chase said, "that's where I'll start."

Andy Clinton stewed and paced in his tiny cubicle. Three steps, turn. Three steps, turn. He hated Chase. Hated him more than anything on Earth. Hated him more than his damn ex-wife. Hated him more than his spoiled-rotten children who took their mother's side on everything. Hated him more than his job and the corrupt bastards who ran the city. He ground his teeth and thought about how good it would feel to kill the son of a bitch. Kill him with his bare hands. He wrung his hands and could almost feel Chase's neck in his grip.

He seethed, remembering the night Cheryl had told him about her affair with Chase. Clinton had met her at a Denny's of all places. He had been hopeful that her agreeing to meet with him was a sign that she was willing to work on their marriage. He had hoped she was going to tell him to move back into the home he had spent a decade paying for. He had wanted desperately to move out of the shitty studio apartment that he had been forced to move into because he couldn't afford anything better while still paying for the house he had been thrown out of. Instead it had been an ambush. Cheryl had told him that she wanted a divorce and had even served him with divorce papers. It had totally blindsided him. He had made a huge mistake when he moved out, thinking that it would wake Cheryl up. He had thought that his leaving would make her realize that she couldn't live without him. He had been wrong.

He begged her not to divorce him. Right there in the middle of Denny's with people all around them. He had even cried. But it did no good. Her mind had been made up. But the biggest bomb of all was yet to come. He couldn't understand why she was so adamant that she was done, and then she told him that she had been hooking up with Chase. While Clinton had been sitting alone in that shitty apartment, eating microwave dinners and frozen pizzas, pining for his wife, Chase had been fucking her.

And now the son of a bitch comes to him, wanting information to help the superstar, nigger basketball player get off for killing a white girl? Bullshit!

Chapter 5

Chase considered his options while driving away from the Beaches' farm. He could head back to Detroit, or he could find Aley's boyfriend. It was an hour drive back to the city; and, as the old saying goes, there's no time like the present. So he set out to find Dan Gentry.

It would have been easy to call Sally and have her do one of those internet searches. She could probably get an address for Gentry in a matter of seconds, but Chase wasn't sure what had happened back there when he had left O'Ryan's. Had she been flirting with him? He needed some time to process it. Besides, how hard could it be to find a man in a town with one stoplight?

A few minutes later he was back in downtown Emerson. It looked exactly as it had the first time he had driven through... deserted. A couple of pickup trucks were parked in front of the Emerson Bar and Grill. Chase parked at the curb in front of the bar. A bumper sticker on the truck he parked behind urged him to re-elect President Bush and Vice-President Quayle.

Inside, the bar resembled the town, dusty and nearly empty. Two old men, who looked like they belonged to the trucks outside, sat at a table in the corner. They followed Chase accusingly with their eyes as he strode to the bar. He didn't take it personally. Any stranger in town would probably have been viewed the same. Hell, any stranger who walked into O'Ryan's would probably be scrutinized by the regulars too.

The bartender, a tall, thin man with an Adam's apple that stuck out almost as far as his weak chin, leaned on the bar, reading the Sunday comics. Chase wondered if he were still trying to get the jokes, or if he simply hadn't had time to get around to reading them. From the looks of the traffic in the bar, he hadn't been too busy.

He looked up from the comics. "What can I do for ya?"

Chase slid onto a vinyl-padded barstool. "How about a beer?"

"Yeah, all right," the bartender muttered, pushing away from his comics.

He moved with the speed and grace of a glacier to the far end of the bar, extracted a longneck bottle from under the counter, popped the cap off with an opener attached to the back wall and moved back toward Chase. At the rate he was moving, the beer would be warm by the time Chase got it.

"My name is Chase," he said as the bartender placed the brown bottle in front of him.

"Good for you," the bartender replied, turning back to his comics.

Chase persevered. "I'm an investigator. I'm trying to find Dan Gentry. I think the lawyer who hired me has some money for him, an inheritance or something along those lines." If he were going to lie, he might as well make it a good one. Saying he was looking for Gentry in connection with the disappearance of his high school girlfriend probably wouldn't get the information he was looking for.

The bartender studied Chase. The eyes of the two old men burned into the back of Chase's skull.

"How come this lawyer don't have Dan's address?"

That was a good question. "I don't know," Chase said, which was the truth. It felt good to tell the truth.

"Seems to me," the bartender continued, "that anyone who wanted to leave some money to Dan would at least have his address."

Seemed logical to Chase as well. He was going to have to work on his lying if he were going to pursue this private investigator thing. He took a drink from the long-neck bottle and shrugged his shoulders. "You know lawyers. They never want to get their hands dirty. They leave all the real work to guys like us." A little camaraderie couldn't hurt.

The bartender didn't respond. He just walked away, back to his comics.

Maybe if Chase helped him understand the comics, the bartender would return the favor and help him out.

"I went to school with Dan."

Chase turned to a kid at the other end of the bar. He sat on a stool, but still gave the impression of height. Long arms rested on the bar. His large hand engulfed the beer bottle he held. He was young but had a full beard.

"Is that right?"

The kid nodded. "Yep. Ol' Dan really had it made. He was captain of all the teams: football, basketball and baseball. He also had the best-lookin' girl: Aley Beach."

"Had? Did they break up or something?"

"Well, Aley went off to college in Detroit. Started hanging out with niggers." He said it as if it was inconceivable, like he was telling Chase that she had been abducted by aliens.

"Really?" Chase said, trying to inject the same inconceivability into his voice.

"Yep." The kid swigged his beer

"Hmm." Chase matched the kid's swig with one of his own. Just two guys drinking beer and shooting the shit. "So Dan took it pretty hard, huh?"

"Sure. Wouldn't you if you knew your girl was fuckin' some nigger?"

"Wait a minute. Are you saying Dan knew that Aley was messing around on him?"

"Sure. This one time she was supposed to come home for this big bonfire we was having, but she didn't show. Dan got all pissed off. Said she was probably off fuckin' her nigger."

"So what did he do?" Chase asked, leaning forward, like he was really getting into the story.

The kid shrugged. "Nothin'. Just got drunk."

"He didn't go get his girl? Bring her back home?"

"Naw. He said, 'Fuck her if that's what she wants.'"

"You believe that?"

"Believe what?"

"That he would just let it go. Just like that?"

"Well, I guess so. Why not?"

"Come on," Chase chided. "Would you let your girl go like that?"

The kid puffed up. "Hell no! I'd kill any nigger that tried to make time with my girl."

"Hey, Bud," one of the old guys called from the corner. "Give us another round here, would ya?"

"Yeah, sure thing," the bartender said.

He moved with the same methodical pace, as if he had to wait for the message to get from his brain to his feet before every step. When he got to the table, one of the old men grabbed him by the front of his shirt and yanked his head down to their level. The two old men whispered a tirade in his ears. When they finally released him, Bud walked back to the bar. He stopped next to the kid and whispered in his ear.

The kid looked at Chase like a chastised third grader. "I'm sorry. I can't talk to you no more."

"But I need to find Dan. Don't you want him to get his money?"

"You better just finish your beer and be on your way," Bud the bartender said.

Chase took his time. He didn't want anyone to think they had run him off. He quietly drank his beer and wondered what, if anything, the small town of Emerson had to do with the disappearance of one of its daughters. Something wasn't right. It prickled at the nape of his neck. He could also still feel the eyes of the two old men burning into the back of his head.

He finished the beer and headed for the door. "See you around, Bud."

He stepped onto the sidewalk outside the bar to find a young man leaning casually against the front fender of the beater pickup truck that had been parked at the Beach farm. He was about six-foot tall with an average build. He wore one of those quilted flannel shirts with blue jeans and work boots and a camouflage ball cap with a Ford logo. His arms were folded across his chest, and his right ankle crossed casually over the left. He was one cool customer.

"I hear you're looking for me," he said with a sneer.

"Dan Gentry?" Chase asked, even though he knew he was talking to the kid from Aley's prom picture.

"That's me."

"I wanted to talk to you about your girlfriend."

"She ain't my girlfriend."

"That's not what her dad said."

"Yeah, well, he don't know."

"He don't, huh?"

Gentry shook his head, not getting the dig. "You working for the nigger?"

"Excuse me? You mean the African-American?"

Gentry scoffed. "African-American, my ass. Half of them can't trace their family to their grandparents, never mind Africa."

"Hmm," Chase said, acting as if he were really thinking about it.

"Whatever," Gentry said. "You're working for the basketball star, Mr. Hotshot Nigger, ain't you?"

"I was asked to help find out what happened to Aley."

"To get the nigger off."

Gentry reached into the bed of the truck. Chase pulled the gun off his hip and had it pointed at the kid before whatever he had in his hand cleared the side of the truck bed.

"Put it down," Chase said.

Gentry's eyes widened when he saw the gun pointed at his chest. He released whatever it was, and it clanged back into the truck bed… obviously, some sort of metal bar. He brought his hand out empty and held it up, along with the other hand.

"Drop the gun!"

Chase turned to see a cop in a two-toned brown uniform pointing a gun of his own. Only this one was pointed at Chase. The officer was in a classic Weaver stance with two hands on the gun, legs shoulder-width apart, front leg slightly bent. His finger was wrapped around the trigger.

Chase lowered his gun to the sidewalk. It was his turn to raise his hands.

Laura Phillips shivered. The temperature hovered around forty. While forty wasn't overly cold, standing outside for three hours in a skirt and open-collar trench coat chilled her to the bone. The bitter wind shooting up her skirt didn't help matters either.

She was the pre-game and post-game host of the Detroit Tigers on Fox Sports Detroit. She should have been able to do her spots on the field and spend the rest of the game in the warmth of the press room or the booth where Mario and Rod sat bundled up with heaters under their desks. She could even do the stupid fan shots from the stands and then hustle her ass back to the warmth, but her pig of a producer wanted her out where she could be seen for the whole game. He said it was good PR for the station. It was also why he insisted that she wear the skirt and open collar. When she had protested, he had said in no uncertain terms that there were a million other girls who would do it if she didn't want to. The fucking pig.

She sat in the camera well next to the dugout. The camera operator, Ritchie, wore a bulky, down-filled parka, a winter hat with a full-face ski mask and thick orange gloves. Her catechism teacher had taught her not to covet her neighbor's goods, but at that moment there was nothing she wanted more in the world than that coat.

"Laura, where are you?"

Laura sighed and answered the producer through her microphone. "In the camera well, next to the dugout."

"I can't see you," he replied through her earpiece. He was in the production truck outside of the stadium. He probably had a cup of coffee to go along with his heater.

"It's cold out here. Why can't I go to the pressroom?"

"How many times do we have to go over this? Sex sells. That's you. We want all the men in the crowd to tell their buddies that they saw you at the game and how sexy you were, so they'll all be watching tomorrow, doing the five-knuckle shuffle."

"Oh, my god," Laura said under her breath. "Fucking pig."

"Why do you let him talk to you like that?" Ritchie said. "You could sue his ass."

"I could. I'd probably even win. But then nobody would touch me. Who's going to hire an on-air reporter who sued her producer?"

"Up," the pig said through the earpiece.

Laura stood slowly and was rewarded with a gust from an Alberta Clipper down the front of her blouse. She sucked in a quick breath. "Holy shit! I think I just lost a nipple."

Ritchie laughed.

"Fuck you and your fucking parka, Ritchie."

Ritchie laughed harder.

Laura turned to give the letches a view. She smiled. "I need to get out of this shithole town." The camera operator in the camera well on the first-base side was pointed at her—the pig keeping her in view.

"And go where?" Ritchie said. "Who's going to hire a chick with only one nipple?"

Laura cut her eyes to Ritchie. He looked intently through the viewfinder of the large camera, aimed at the pitcher. She laughed. She knew it was a joke. Ritchie was a good guy. Not at all like the pig.

"I need a story," she said. "Something big. Not that old Mrs. Sourpuss-who-watched-Ty-Cobb-play bullshit."

"What about the Bowe Bradlee thing."

"What Bowe Bradlee thing?"

Chapter 6

Chase spent the night in a jail cell, staring at a water stain on the ceiling with a mattress spring pushing against his shoulder. He couldn't sleep. His thoughts were filled with Sally. Of course, he thought she was beautiful and a great person, but he had never thought that she had thought that way about him. And what if it didn't work out? They saw each other every day. How awkward would that be? And there was that whole thing with her being Sarge's niece. How would he react?

Sleep finally found him sometime in the early-morning hours.

He woke a few hours later to a voice saying, "Well, what do you want me to do with him? All right. All right. I'll take care of it." It was followed by a clatter of plastic, instantly recognized for someone from Chase's generation as a plastic telephone handset being returned to the base's cradle. He hadn't heard that sound in a long time. It had been years since he had even seen that style of phone.

Chase swung his feet to the floor and sat up on the bed. The guy who he assumed had been talking on the phone sat at an old wood desk with pointy-toed cowboy boots crossed at the ankles on the desk. He was solidly built with a bad haircut and wore the same uniform as the kid who had arrested Chase the day before.

The guy saw him looking. He swung his feet off the desk and walked to the cell. "On your feet."

Chase stood. "I have a license for the gun and a permit to carry it."

The cop's hand shot through the bars as fast as lightening, grabbed the front of Chase's shirt and yanked. Chase hadn't seen it coming and couldn't get his hands up in time to stop the momentum. He did manage to turn his head just before the bars crashed into the right side of his face. Stars filled his vision, just like Bugs Bunny when he got whacked in the head.

"Not in my town," the cop hissed. The name plate on his uniform said "Bradshaw." "We don't like people snooping around here."

"Why? You have something to hide?"

Chase knew it was a mistake as soon as he'd said it. With the speed of a viper strike, Bradshaw pushed him away from the cell bars and yanked him back into them.

"We don't like smart asses either."

"I'll keep that in mind," Chase said. A welt had already started to swell on the side of his head.

"You do that. Now here's what we're going to do. I'm going to take you back to your car and follow you out of town. You are *not* going to come back. If you do, I won't be as nice as I was this time."

Chase had been wrong after all. They were going to run him off.

Clinton sat in Lieutenant Dick Northern's office. Northern was one of the only other white men in the department that he could talk to. The fact that Northern hated Chase almost as much as he did didn't hurt. They had both loathed the press Chase had gotten following the Woodstock thing, Northern especially. He had worked hard to get Chase thrown out of the department. To see him doing well and becoming famous to boot had really burned him up.

"I have to get this fucking kid, Dick," Clinton said. "Send his black ass to jail with the rest of his kind."

Northern looked non-committal, but Clinton knew he felt the same way. The chance to take down a high-profile black kid and take Chase down a notch or two at the same time was too good an opportunity to pass on.

"What have you got?"

"I've got a missing white girl, last seen with the black kid."

"That's it?"

"Pretty much."

"Who said she was with the basketball player?"

"Her roommate."

"Have you corroborated it?"

Clinton felt his face flush a little. "Well, no."

Northern scowled. "What have you been doing?"

Clinton started to respond, but Northern rolled his eyes and held up his hand to stop him. "Never mind. You have to get someone to corroborate that the missing girl was with Bradlee. Until then, it's his word against hers. And in this town... "

"They all stick together," Clinton said with scorn.

Chapter 7

Chase returned to O'Ryan's just in time to miss the morning rush. Timing is everything.

Sally hadn't made it in yet either so Sarge was alone, looking harried and irritated.

"Hey, Denzel!" one of the usual drunks called as Chase walked through the door. Chase ignored him. He was too tired.

"Where the hell were you?" Sarge said.

"Jail."

"Yeah, right."

Chase made a beeline for the coffee pot. "Whatever. I don't have the energy to argue with you."

He waited until Sally arrived. Nobody else came into the bar during that time, but he felt bad about leaving Sarge alone, even though he thought Sarge had overreacted, so Chase helped him clean up.

"Were you really in jail?" Sarge asked as they filled empty cardboard beer cases with empty bottles.

"Yep. In a little town called Emerson." He went on to tell Sarge about the small, one-stoplight town. About the Beaches' hundred-year-old farm. About the Emerson Bar and about the confrontation with Aley's boyfriend and his subsequent arrest.

Sarge listened intently and then said, "They seem to have overreacted."

Chase chuckled to himself. Sarge saying they overreacted was the pot calling the kettle black, but he didn't say it. Instead he said, "That's kind of what I thought."

"Well, you did pull a gun on the kid."

"The kid was going to bash my skull in with a crowbar."

"Yeah, there is that," Sarge conceded. "But why do you

think they overreacted like they did?"

Chase hadn't figured that out yet. "I don't know."

"What's it have to do with the missing girl?"

"I don't know that either."

Sally finally appeared and went straight to the back room without saying "good morning," "go to hell" or anything. Chase didn't know what to say to her either, so he didn't. He headed over to the D State campus.

He started with the resident advisor at Aley's dorm. The RA was a snotty, arrogant, twenty-two-year-old grad student. He had a ponytail and round glasses. He was probably getting his master's in philosophy or something stupid like that. Chances were good that he was headed for a career as a middle school social studies teacher, if he were lucky. Maybe the RA knew it as well, and that was why he had such a shitty attitude... or he was just a douche bag. Sometimes Chase gave people too much credit.

He wanted to throw the kid through a wall when he said, "I'm not a babysitter."

He didn't because the kid was right. Dammit.

"So you don't have any idea where she could be? She never talked to you about anything that could help find her?"

"No. I tried to talk to her back in the fall when she first moved in. She is a typical freshman, immature."

Translation: he tried to get in her pants, and she shot him down.

Chase had a little more luck with Aley's roommate, Rachel Corrigan. They sat in the dorm lobby on green vinyl couches that had been new sometime in the seventies. She wore black yoga pants and a gray sweatshirt that said "St. Mary's Track" across the front. Her hair was pulled back in a ponytail, revealing a high, round forehead. Combined with big round eyes and a small pointed nose, she looked like an animated bird from a children's book.

"I already talked to the other cop."

Chase didn't give away the fact that he wasn't a cop. "I know. I just want to hear it for myself. So please, tell me what happened."

"There's not much to tell. There was a party over at the University Towers. The basketball team had won a big game, and they were celebrating. Aley and I went. I came home early. I had a headache."

"And Aley didn't come home at all?"

Rachel shook her head.

"And that didn't alarm you?"

She looked at Chase as if he were naive. "It wasn't the first time she hadn't come home."

"Oh, sure," Chase said, trying to be cool. "So what's the rumor about her being last seen with Bowe Bradlee?"

Rachel looked away. "I've heard that."

"Detective Clinton said that you told him that."

"I saw the two of them talking. And... I saw them heading towards Bowe's bedroom."

"And that's the last you saw of her?"

"Yes."

"And now she's missing."

"And Bowe, from what I hear."

"So what? You think they ran off together?"

The future social studies teacher had been hovering. He said, "Bowe Bradlee was accused of rape a couple of years ago."

"Go away, Todd," Rachel said. "Bowe didn't rape Aley."

"How do you know?" Todd said.

"Because I know Aley. He wouldn't have had to rape her, especially as drunk as she was."

"That's nice," Chase said.

"Well, it's true!"

"Go away, Todd," Chase said.

Todd wanted to stay. His eyes gave it away, but he just

didn't have it in him to defy Chase.

When he left, Rachel rolled her eyes and said, "He's creepy. He's always hitting on all the girls."

"What's his batting average?"

"Uh, zero," she said as if it should have been obvious.

Chase laughed and then got back to business. "Detective Clinton said Aley's suitcase is missing?"

"Yes. I didn't notice it right away, but when her mom called to say that she couldn't get ahold of her, well, that's when I noticed that the suitcase was gone."

"And that was unusual? Other times when she stayed out all night she didn't take it?"

"Not that I ever saw."

Chase nodded. "Okay. Was there anything else she was involved in that might have anything to do with her disappearance?"

"Like what?"

"Anything. Was she involved with a teacher who might have been married? Was she into drugs? Was she suicidal? Was she going out at night to feed the homeless?"

Rachel laughed. "Feed the homeless?"

Chase smiled. "So, no to the philanthropy?"

"Uh, no. Aley was pretty much only concerned with Aley."

"Was she doing drugs?"

Rachel looked away. "Not that I know of."

Chase didn't believe her. "Really?"

"Really," Rachel said, trying too hard to convince him.

"So if I were to ask the other residents here, they would back that up?"

Rachel sighed heavily. "Okay. Maybe she had gotten into some of that stuff."

"Was she in deep?"

Rachel looked away. "Pretty deep, I guess."

"Do you know where she was getting it?"

"No," Rachel said adamantly.

Chase gave her his best cop look. He could look mean when he wanted to.

"I swear I don't know."

"Do you know a girl named Meghan McAllister?"

Rachel thought for a second. "I don't... wait, is that the girl from Aley's hometown?"

"Yes, that's her."

"I don't know her. I just know Aley has hitched rides back and forth with her a few times. Why?"

"I'm just trying to find Aley. Do you know where Meghan lives?"

"No, sorry."

Chase nodded his head and stood. He pointed at the sweatshirt. "St. Mary's in Monroe?"

"Huh?" Rachel looked down at her chest where Chase pointed. "Oh, no, Port Huron."

"Nice area," Chase said, doing his best Jim Price.

"I guess."

The sun had finally made an appearance, and the temperature hovered in the mid-fifties. For the first time that season, Laura wasn't covered in goose bumps. Since it was a day game, she hoped that the temps would rise even higher throughout the game, rather than drop as they did during the night games. She sat in the dugout next to the pig. It was her least favorite part of the job. It was bad enough to have to talk to him through the microphone, but to sit next to him made her skin crawl.

They went over plans for that day's game. The pre-game would be a review of last night's win. She had interviewed the winning pitcher, Jordan Zimmerman, and they would show that. They were also planning to show a recording of a trip she had taken to the children's hospital with Justin Verlander. It would be an easy day. All she'd really have to do is set up the two clips. The guys in the studio would

40

handle the rest.

With that decided, the pig changed the subject. "I've arranged for you to meet tomorrow with a public relations officer from the Detroit Police. We want to do a story on the new Police Athletic League facility that they're trying to build over at the site of the old stadium. I'll email the details to you."

More fluff, but that was her job. "Okay, sounds good."

The pig stood to leave. Laura called him back. "I was wondering if I could run something else by you."

"Sure. What's up?"

"I'm hearing rumors that there is a girl missing from over at D State and that Bowe Bradlee might be connected to it somehow."

The pig raised his eyebrows and cocked his head to the side. "And?"

Laura took a breath and steadied herself. "And I'd like to look into it."

"Look into it?"

"Yeah. You know, investigate. Like a real reporter."

The pig laughed. He grabbed his chin between his thumb and index finger in an exaggerated imitation of deep thought. "Let's see. First, if you haven't noticed, we are a baseball show, not basketball. Second, you're not a real reporter. You're a pretty face that we use to attract viewers."

"But I thought—"

"We don't pay you to think, Laura."

Chapter 8

Chase didn't know what to think about the information he had obtained. The sun was out, and the temperature had passed fifty for the first time. The Tigers had an afternoon game scheduled with the Astros. Maybe he could get his thoughts together at the ball game.

He parked on John R a few blocks north of Comerica Park. As he walked to the stadium, he remembered the first time he had ever been to a game. His father had taken him to the old park Tigers Stadium to see his hometown heroes play the Kansas City Royals. The core of the '84 team was in the process of breaking into the big leagues, and they were still a few years away from greatness.

Tigers Stadium had sat on the corner of Michigan and Trumbull for a hundred years, a great white whale in the middle of the city. It looked impenetrable from the outside, made from concrete and steel like a Civil War fort. Entering the grand stadium had consisted of endlessly walking up ramp after concrete ramp amid the steel skeleton of the structure. When they finally reached the upper deck and walked through the tunnel to the stands, the view had taken Chase's breath away.

The colors had been so vivid. It was like when Dorothy had stepped through the front door of her house from a land of black and white to one of color. The sun blazed in the bluest sky he had ever seen. It was impossible that it was the same sky that hung outside the stadium. The green of the grass was a vivid contrast to the weed-infested empty lots that dotted Detroit. And the infield dirt had an orange tint that Mother Nature had never created.

Some of the best days of his life had been spent in the old ballpark, first with his dad in the upper-deck reserved seats and later with his buddies in the bleachers. Back in high school, they could get bleacher seats for four bucks. It was cheaper than going to the movies.

Sadly, the old place had been torn down and replaced with a brand new, sleek, state-of-the-art stadium, Comerica Park. It was open and airy and afforded a view of downtown past the outfield bleachers. It was possibly the most beautiful place he had ever been to watch a ball game, but it wasn't Tigers Stadium.

Chase sat in the bleachers next to an old man wearing a 1968 Al Kaline replica road jersey and a hat with the Tigers famous old English D on the front. The hat wasn't a replica. It had been worn by Kaline at some point during the '68 season. The story of how the old man had come to possess the hat was still a little fuzzy after all of these years, but he swore he had gotten it from the Hall of Famer himself.

"How's it going, Dad?" Chase said.

The old man was methodically working his way through a bag of peanuts, the shells in a mound between his feet. "Same," he said, not looking at his son.

He had retired from the Detroit Police several years prior and had taken up residence in the bleachers at Comerica Park. He had spent his entire adult life in a patrol car, never having the desire to further his career. He had felt it was the best way to serve and protect. He thought it more important to stop the crime before it took place. In his mind all detectives, like his son, did was clean up the mess after peoples' lives had been ruined. He had wanted to stop the crime before it had happened; and, in his estimation, you had to be on the street to do that.

He was the most decent person Chase had ever met. Working a patrol car for an entire career wouldn't make a person rich by any stretch of the imagination, but he hadn't done it for the money. Chase respected the hell out of his father and strived every day to be more like him.

"I miss anything?" Chase said, having missed the first inning.

"Can you not see that 200-foot-wide scoreboard over there?"

Chase looked at the massive screen behind the left-field stands. No runs, no hits, no errors for either team. Anibal Sanchez toed the rubber for the Tigers. Dallas Kuechel for the Astros. There probably wouldn't be many runs scored that day.

"You still got that hat?"

"Damn straight." The old man cracked open another peanut, letting the shells fall to the pile and then shucked the red skins off the two nuts and threw them into his mouth. It was the exact procedure he had employed for eating peanuts since Chase could remember. "Best player on the best team in Tigers history," he said while chewing.

"Kaline didn't play on the '84 Tigers," Chase said, reigniting the argument they'd been having for thirty years.

"That's why I said the *best* team in Tigers history. Those '84 bums couldn't hold a candle to the '68 team."

"Bums? Gibson, Morris, Parrish, Tram and Lou—"

The old man snorted. "Bums. Every one of 'em. Probably wouldn't have even made the team in '68."

And so it went for several innings. Chase and his dad argued '68 versus '84 while a guy a few rows ahead of them heckled the Astros right fielder with, "Hey Springer! My girlfriend plays right field too!" and the like, and Sanchez and Kuechel both worked their ways through the opposing line-ups with relative ease. It was familiar and comfortable. Baseball hadn't changed in a hundred years.

The old man finally ended the argument in the seventh inning. "I hear you're looking into a missing girl."

"Where'd you hear that?"

"I still have ears in the department."

"I know you do," Chase said. He told his dad about Aley

44

Beach and Bowe Bradlee. He told him about the changes the girl had gone through during her year at D State and her alleged use of drugs.

"She was into drugs?"

"Sounds like it."

"Those drugs are bad business. I thank God every day that you stayed out of that mess. I was you, I'd look into that angle."

The Tigers bullpen blew Sanchez's gem in the top of the eighth when Houston's right fielder hit a three-run home run into the bushes in straight away center. He smiled broadly at the heckler when he returned to the outfield. "Your girlfriend do that?"

Chase had eaten three hotdogs, drunk two beers and gotten mustard on his shirt, but he hadn't figured out where Aley Beach was. The only things he knew for sure was that she hadn't played for the Tigers or the Astros.

He returned to O'Ryan's. He slid onto a stool at the bar and looked at Sally's butt. God was on his game the day he had created it. She should have been a jeans model instead of hanging around a cop bar in Detroit.

She spun on him. "What are you looking at?"

"Nothing," Chase lied.

"How's your dad?"

"How do you know I saw my dad?"

"You have mustard on your shirt."

Chase looked down at the yellow spot on his chest. "Oh, right. He's the same. Still delusional."

"Still thinks the '68 Tigers were better than '84?"

Chase shook his head. "Crazy old man."

"You look like a confused dog," Sally said.

"I do?"

She nodded. "Like your owner pulled the fake throwing-the-ball trick."

"Hmm." It was how he felt, but he didn't know it

showed. "What are you confused about?"

"The suitcase."

"What suitcase?"

"The suitcase that's missing from Aley Beach's dorm room."

"So what has you confused?"

"Clinton says the missing suitcase indicates that Aley left of her own volition."

Sally nodded. "Makes sense."

"Sure," Chase replied, "but if she were going away for a few days, she would have been back by now. But if she weren't planning on coming back... "

"She would have taken *all* of her clothes," Sally said, tuning into the confusion.

They sat in silence for a minute. Sun streamed through the port hole in the outside door. Dust motes floated in the rays.

Sally broke the silence. "So what does it mean?"

"Hell if I know."

Chapter 9

Mrs. Beach sent Meghan McAllister's school address to Chase the next morning so, as soon as the morning rush had been served and cleaned up, he drove to the campus to pay her a visit. She lived in a dorm similar to Aley's, complete with the green-painted cement-block walls and industrial tile floors. Chase went through the same sequence as he had to meet with Rachel Corrigan, but this resident advisor was cool—must have been a criminal-justice major. He went and got Meghan without the attitude and allowed Chase to meet with her in the lobby alone.

The vinyl-cushioned couch he sat on was identical to the one in Aley's dorm lobby, as was the coffee table and the arm chair that Meghan McAllister sat in. She, however, was very different from Rachel Corrigan.

She was a year older and a decade more mature. She wore blue jeans and a flannel shirt with the sleeves turned back. Her eyes were green and focused. Her hair was a deep, rich red and straight, parted in the middle like Marcia Brady. She had freckles on her neck that flowed under the collar of her shirt. She probably had freckles on her face as well and hated them, but her face was caked with makeup and none showed. As a kid, she had probably been teased about the freckles by boys who would one day grow up to realize just how sexy they actually were, at least in Chase's opinion. Life can be funny sometimes. You live your whole life thinking that something is a defect when actually it's one of your best traits. She wore no jewelry, hair clips or any other accessories. A cup of coffee sat on the wooden armrest of her chair. A tendril of steam rose from the cup.

"I'm looking for Aley Beach," Chase said.

Meghan's eyes widened just a bit. "Is she missing?"

"You don't know?"

"We're not exactly friends."

"But you give her rides back and forth to school."

Meghan nodded. "Aley's mom asked my mom to ask me. I said 'yes.' It's really not that big of a deal. But I really don't know what she does here on campus or at home, for that matter. We just don't run in the same circles."

"So if she were to go missing… "

"I really wouldn't know."

"Did the two of you talk in the car? It's about an hour's drive, right?"

"It is, but not really. The first few trips we talked. Aley asked me questions about life on campus and that sort of thing. But as the first semester went on, she sort of changed. I think she was more into partying than school."

"Do you know if she were using drugs?"

Meghan scowled her disapproval. "She mentioned marijuana once. I told her I wasn't interested, and that was pretty much it."

"So if she had been using, you wouldn't know where she got it?"

"Oh, god no," Meghan gasped. "I mean, I'm sure I could probably find drugs if I wanted to, but I don't want to."

"And you haven't heard from her since… "

She thought back. "It's been a while actually. I texted her the week before last to tell her I was heading home for the weekend and see if she wanted to go. She never responded."

Chase sighed. This was going nowhere. "Okay."

Meghan looked concerned. "She's really missing?"

"She seems to be."

"Are her parents okay?"

"I don't think so."

The corner of Michigan and Trumbell is perhaps the most famous historical spot in Detroit. To Tigers fans, it is hallowed ground. It is the site where the Detroit Tigers played baseball from 1912 until 1999, under the guises Navin Field, Briggs Stadium and Tiger Stadium. It is the place where Ty Cobb won twelve batting titles in a thirteen-year span, where Al Kaline hit 226 of his 399 career homeruns and the place that the 1935, 1945, 1968 and 1984 World Champions called home.

Laura Phillips stood on the corner in a skirt and heels. Her back was to the field which, despite the fact that the stadium no longer stood, looked ready to host a game. The lot had been empty since the stadium came down, but residents of the Corktown area, as well as a group calling themselves The Navin Field Grounds Crew had kept the field itself in pristine condition.

The sun shone and the temperature hovered in the low fifties. A crisp breeze blew across Laura's legs and ruffled the skirt. She was there to do the story on the new Police Athletic League program called Kids at The Corner. She interviewed both the PAL director and a PR officer from the DPD. She led them through the basics of the program which would include a multisport complex for the kids, in addition to the ball field. It would also give the PAL a permanent home.

When everybody was happy with the shot, the cameraman went about packing up his equipment, and the PAL director hurried off to wherever it was a PAL director spent his days— soon it would be right there. Laura grabbed the PR officer before he could get away.

He was tall and black with an easy smile and very white teeth. He was formally dressed in a full, dark-blue uniform. He wore no coat and didn't appear to be cold. His name was Woods. Laura had never dealt with him personally but dealing with reporters was his job, and he didn't seem to mind when she asked him for one more minute.

Laura took a breath and thought for the 1,000th time if

she should ask what she was about to ask. The pig had made it clear that he didn't want her pursuing this. Did she really want to put her job on the line? On the other hand, did she really want to keep the job? She let the breath out and jumped in. "I'm hearing rumblings that Bowe Bradlee is involved in a girl's disappearance."

Woods continued to smile. He looked off in the distance. The Motown Casino stood tall on the horizon. He smoothed his mustache with his thumb and index finger and then looked back at Laura. "Officially, the department has no comment on any case involving Bowe Bradlee."

"What about unofficially?"

Woods looked at the cameraman loading the camera into the back of the news van. "Off the record?"

"Yes."

"A girl has been reported missing. She was last seen at a party that Bowe Bradlee had also attended."

"So is Bowe a suspect? A person of interest?"

"Bowe is a basketball player and probably going to be the number-one pick in the NBA draft. He is a product of the very Police Athletic League that we're here to talk about today. Imagine the boost it would give our campaign for a local boy, a product of the PAL, to go number one in the NBA draft."

Laura returned Officer Woods' smile. "So he's not a suspect because of the PR you can get from him?"

"I didn't say that. All I know at this point is that he was at the same party the missing girl was at... as were several other people. I see the look in your eyes, Miss Phillips. You think I'm covering up Bowe's involvement because of who he is and what he can mean for our project here, but think about this: if you were to throw Bowe's name out there as a suspect just because he's Bowe Bradlee, the presumptive number-one pick, how would that make you any different than me?"

The van door slammed shut. "Laura, let's go," the cameraman called.

Laura ignored him. "Is there anybody looking for the girl?"

"Of course. You have to understand, though, with all the murders, car-jackings and other violent crimes that are daily occurrences in this city, the disappearance of an adult is not a high priority."

The van horn honked.

"You're going to miss your ride," Woods said.

Laura held a hand up to the cameraman. "He'll wait. Who has the case?"

Chapter 10

It took a couple of calls to friends and old colleagues who would still talk to him, but Chase finally tracked down one of his old snitches to a strip club on the southeast side of town. Several cars and trucks that looked as much a part of southeast Detroit as the burned-out houses and empty lots were parked in a parking lot that was missing more asphalt than it actually had. The neon sign bolted to the roof said "Lucky's" and promised nude girls and ice cold beer. While the two were normally not a bad combination, Chase wasn't feeling very optimistic, based on the neighborhood and the building itself.

He paid the cover to a doorman roughly the size of the Renaissance Center and stepped into Lucky's. Spotlights pointed at the stage and a disco ball that twirled from the ceiling, bouncing light around the room. "American Woman" by Lenny Kravitz blared from the sound system while a young lady somewhere between fifteen and fifty-five worked her ass off on the stage. Unfortunately, she had plenty of ass to work with. With all due respect to Sir Mix-A-Lot, Chase did not "like big butts," at least not ones with cellulite dimples that made it look like a golf ball.

The sign on the roof was right about the nude girls; they were everywhere. It was just good that it hadn't promised pretty nude girls; that would have been a lie. When he was fourteen years old, nobody would have convinced Chase that one day he wouldn't want to see a lady, any lady, without clothes on. Looking around Lucky's, he saw several that he would have gladly purchased clothes for just to cover them up.

"You know Slick Rick?" he asked the doorman, holding a twenty up where he could see it.

The bill disappeared into the man's giant fist. He pointed to a booth in a dark corner on the other side of the room. Chase weaved through people and tables, trying not to touch anything and trying to ignore the sucking sound his shoes made on the sticky floor.

He found a man in a booth in the dark corner. His head was tipped back on the back rest, eyes closed, mouth open. The naked young lady curled on the seat next to him seemed to be doing something with her hands below the table. Chase had arrived just in time for the happy ending. The young lady kissed her customer on the cheek and withdrew from the booth.

"Really?" Chase said.

Slick Rick jumped and banged his knees on the underside of the table as he jerked back to reality. "What the fuck?"

"My sentiments exactly," Chase said. He checked the bench seat opposite Rick to ensure he wouldn't sit in something that he'd regret and slid into the booth, consciously keeping his legs from touching the underside of the table.

Rick was thin and pale to the point that he nearly glowed when the disco-ball lights hit him. Dirty blond hair hung to his skinny shoulders. He had gages in his ears, and a hoop nose- ring pierced his right nostril.

"Chase," he said when the blood had made it back to his head. "You scared the shit outta me. What are you doing here?"

"You old enough to be in a place like this?" The first time they had met, Rick hadn't yet dropped out of high school. He had been caught with marijuana in his locker. It wasn't enough that the prosecutor would have even brought charges, but Rick hadn't known that. Chase told him he'd get him out of trouble if he'd become a snitch.

"Yes, I am. You wanna see my ID?"

Chase shook his head. "Damn, I'm getting old."

"What?"

"Nothing. You know, they have places like this that actually have attractive women in them."

Rick grinned like the teenager he had first met. "I know, but those girls don't give the same services as the girls here do."

Chase flashed back to the scene he had stumbled upon. "Oh, right."

"So what are you doing here, Chase?"

"I just came to say 'hi.' See how you're doing."

"Bullshit."

"Okay, you're right. I need some information."

"Fuck you, man. I heard you're not even a cop anymore. I don't have to talk to you."

"You're right, Rick," Chase said. "You don't have to talk to me. I just thought I'd buy you a beer, and you'd answer my question for old time's sake."

"What question?"

"Who supplies D State?"

Rick laughed. "Keep your money. I'll buy my own beer."

"That bad?"

"I'm done with this conversation," Rick said, shaking his head.

"This is important, Rick."

"Uh-uh, fuck you."

Rick started to slide out of the booth. Chase reached out and grabbed a handful of the greasy hair. He yanked and bent Rick in half backwards. The skinny shoulders lay flat on the table. His legs caught between the table and the seat, wedging him into an agonizing position.

"I'm afraid I'm going to have to insist."

Rick clawed at Chase's hand and wrist. "I want nothing to do with those guys."

"Who?" Chase said, pulling on the hoop in his nose with his other hand.

"The BD Boyz!"

Chase let go of the nose ring and the greasy hair and pushed Rick off the table. He flopped back onto the bench seat. He sat up slowly, grabbing at his lower back.

"Those guys still around?" Chase said. "I thought that place was empty." BD stood for Brewster-Douglass, the Federal housing project downtown.

Rick nodded. "It is, except for the BD Boyz."

"Who's running them now?"

"You don't know?" Rick said incredulously.

"That's why I'm asking."

"Atari Black." Rick waited for Chase to recognize the name.

"Am I supposed to know that name?"

"Christ, you are out of the game. He's Bowe Bradlee's brother."

"You've got to be shittin' me."

Chase left Lucky's feeling very unlucky. He had a girl on drugs, last seen with the brother of the guy supplying the drugs. Throw in the fact that the drug supplier happened to be running the most dangerous street gang in one of the most dangerous cities in the country, and you get a volatile mix of shit.

He drove back to the campus and entered the college police station. The chief of the D State police was an old comrade, Dennis Harden. Harden had reached the rank of Commander in the DPD and had retired when his current position presented itself. He still came into O'Ryan's now and again to hang out with the rest of the bums.

The lobby of the station was separated from the area where the police officers worked by a half-wall made of concrete and painted a dark green. Bullet-proof glass filled the opening from the top of the wall to the ceiling. Chase had to talk to the desk sergeant through one of those intercom/air vent things like at the gas station. The fact that the police had barricaded themselves from the city that they were supposed to be protecting the kids from didn't escape him. He was a trained detective after all.

He spoke into the intercom thing. "I need to talk to Dennis Harden, please."

"The chief?" the cop sitting behind the glass said. She was a young black woman with beautiful brown eyes. Chase happened to notice that she wasn't wearing a bullet-proof vest by the way her uniform blouse clung to her figure. Her voice through the intercom sounded like a female Darth Vader.

"Is there another Dennis Harden here?"

"No."

"Then yes, the chief."

The young lady's eyes weren't nearly as beautiful when they scowled. She stood and walked away without a word. The view from the back was every bit as good as the view from the front. She returned a minute later with Harden in tow. He saw Chase through the glass and laughed. He said something to the desk cop, and they both laughed.

What was that all about?

Harden was black too, but that was where the similarities with the desk cop stopped. He was of average height with a slightly-above-average paunch. He wore his hair in a moderate
Afro, and he had a thick black mustache. He looked like a '90s era sitcom dad. He wore a mint-green uniform shirt and darker green pants with a mint-green stripe on the outside of each leg.

He pulled an ID card attached to one of those retractable strings and pressed it to a card reader. The door unlocked with a *whir* and a *chunk*. Harden pulled it open and waved Chase through.

Chase stepped though the opening. "Hey, Dennis. What's with the Boy Scout uniform?"

"Boy Scouts don't wear green. They wear brown."

"Girl Scouts?"

Harden didn't answer. He walked back the way he had come. He must have trained the girl at the desk.

Chase followed Harden into a small office where the chief flopped into a chair behind a small desk barely big enough to conceal his lower body.

"I know you're not dumb enough to come here and insult me prior to asking for a favor. So what do you want?"

"Insult you?" Chase said. "C'mon, buddy. That's what friends do."

"What do you want, Chase?"

"A favor."

Harden laughed and rubbed his eyes. "You're a piece a work."

Chase sat in a chair facing the desk. "I'm looking into the disappearance of one of your students."

Harden nodded. "Aley Beach."

"That's the one."

"I'm not really involved in it. We're cooperating with the DPD of course, but it's their case."

"You're not looking for her?"

Harden sat up in his chair and leaned forward. "Look, Chase. This isn't easy to say, but we're just a campus police force. My guys spend their days breaking up parties and writing parking tickets. Me, I was a traffic cop my whole career. Yes, I made it to commander, but it was in traffic. We simply don't have the know-how to investigate a missing-persons case."

"Are you done with the *mea culpa?*"

"What?"

"I didn't come here to ask you to help me find her, Dennis," Chase said and then corrected himself. "Well, actually I did, but not in that way."

"So what do you want?"

"Drugs."

"Wait, what? You want drugs?"

"No, drugs are the topic. Do you have kids doing drugs?"

"Of course. This is a college campus. Drugs and alcohol are common."

"It sounds like you're okay with it."

Harden rolled his eyes. "No, I am not okay with it. But it's reality. There's something like twenty-million drug users in this country. It stands to reason that some of them are going to be on my campus. Do I like it? Condone it? Of course not. If we catch them, we deal with it."

"Who are the dealers?"

"Right now?" He shook his head. "I don't know. If we catch the dealers, we expel them from the university. But, as long as there's a demand, someone will supply it."

"Do you ask the kids you catch who their dealer is?"

"Of course, we do. They don't tell us, and they know we don't have the authority to make them."

Chase smiled. "I bet I can get it out of them."

"You have less authority than I do."

"Wanna bet?"

Harden sat back in the chair and studied Chase through squinted eyes. "What's the bet?"

"If I can't get a name, you drink free for a month at O'Ryan's."

Harden nodded his head and smiled. "Now you're talking."

"But when I *do* get a name, you give me whatever I need when it comes to this case."

Harden continued to nod. "How many of my kids do you get to rough up?"

"I only need one."

"Bet," Harden said, slapping his hand on the desk. "I've got just the name for you."

Clinton hit the street in search of evidence. He hadn't

really done it in a while, but he was on a mission. With retirement looming, it would be nice to go out on a high. This case was his chance to do so. Maybe he could write his memoirs and make some money.

He started in the dorm where the girl was last seen, storming up and down the corridors, banging on doors and barking questions at whoever answered. Most of the residents hadn't been at the party and didn't even know of the girl. Some had heard the news of a missing girl but knew no details. By the time he got to the floor that the basketball players lived on, he was beyond frustrated.

He slammed his meaty fist on the cheap, plywood door of the first room he came to. In the world of Mixed Martial Arts that Clinton loved to watch—it was a human cock fight, he loved to watch the dumb asses beat the shit out of each other, and now they let girls do it, it was almost better than porn— it's called a hammer fist. The door opened, and a tall black kid stripped to the waist scowled down at him. His upper body was covered in tattoos like the graffiti his people sprayed all over the abandoned buildings downtown. The kid was obviously a basketball player. He was several inches taller than Clinton but looked like the stick figures his kids used to draw. His mama probably spent all the welfare money on crack instead of groceries.

The kid looked angry. He also looked like he had just gotten out of bed, unless fucked-up was a hair style now. "Whatchu want, man?"

Clinton flashed his badge.

The kid was unimpressed. "So? That supposed to mean something to me?"

"What's your name?"

"I ain't gotta tell you shit!"

"Why so hostile?"

"Hey, fuck you! I don't need 5-0 up here banging on my damn door."

"Now you did it," Clinton said. He placed his hand on the kid's chest and pushed him into the dorm room. It didn't take much with how skinny the kid was. Clinton stepped in and shut the door.

The kid stumbled backward into a small living room. A beat-to-hell, brown leather couch sat against one wall. A wide- screen TV hung on the wall opposite. In between, floor-to-ceiling windows opened onto a spectacular view of Canada.

"You can't do that!"

"I just did."

"Don't you need a warrant or something?"

Clinton chuckled. "Apparently not. Now, what's your name?"

The basketball player stood defiantly, not speaking. Clinton wanted to punch him in the face.

"I can find out," he said, "but it would make me very happy if you just told me. It would set the tone for a relationship of cooperation."

The kid still didn't speak. His jaw was clenched tight. Veins stood out on his skinny neck.

It was Clinton's turn to be unimpressed. "I can find out one of two ways. I can find the resident advisor, or I can go through your stuff until I find something with your name on it. I think I'll do the latter; that means the second option," he explained in a condescending tone. He started toward a closed bedroom door. "Is this your room? Is there anything in it you don't want 5-0 to find?"

The kid cracked. "Deon Henderson."

Clinton stopped and turned back. "Now was that so hard?" Now that Deon Henderson had cracked, it would be easier. "That was the easy question. They're going to get harder. For instance, do you know Bowe Bradlee?"

"Yeah."

"Good. Now we're getting somewhere. Were you at the

party in his room the night you guys won your conference tournament?"

"Yeah."

"Did you see Bradlee there?"

"It was his room."

"Yes, but did you *see* him?"

Deon shrugged. "I guess so."

Clinton produced a picture and held it out. "Did you see him with this girl?"

Deon barely looked at the photo. "I don't know."

Clinton stepped close and pushed the kid down onto the couch. It's hard to intimidate someone who is almost a foot taller than you. He held the picture close to Deon's face. "Look at it."

"I don't know," Deon whined. "I might have. I don't know."

Clinton shook his head. He turned and headed back toward the bedroom door.

Deon called after him. "Wait!"

Damn! What did that kid have in that room?

"You want me to say I saw her there? Fine, I saw her there."

Clinton stepped back to the couch and leaned over, putting his face inches from Deon's. "And she was with Bradlee?"

Deon's face twisted in agony. He looked over Clinton's shoulder at the bedroom door. "Fine," he said. "She was with Bowe."

Clinton turned to leave. "I'll be back," he said.

As he turned the doorknob, Deon Henderson said, "Why you doing this?"

Clinton turned back. "I'm just doing my job."

"What about that other cop?"

"What other cop?"

"The one who's been asking around campus about that girl in the picture."

61

Clinton was incensed. He had told that fucking Chase to back off. He'd just have to remind the asshole. This time he'd make sure his message got through.

Chapter 11

The name Harden had given Chase was Anthony Douglas. Chase caught up with him in the corridor outside the weight room. Douglas was a backup defensive lineman on the D State football team. The program listed him at six-three and 280 pounds. He had no neck. His trapezius muscles extended from his ears to bowling-ball-sized shoulders. From the gigantic shoulders hung tree-trunk-sized arms covered in tattoos that were hard to read against his dark skin. The kid was a black, tatted-up Arnold Schwarzenegger with a bald head and gold teeth. And he was a backup? What did the starters look like?

Sweat beaded on Douglas' bald dome, and veins the size of snakes stood out on his massive arms. He bobbed his head to a beat that leaked between his ears and the headphones that weren't big enough to cover them. He held a gallon of chocolate milk in his hand. Chase had heard that chocolate milk was the new fad in post-workout replenishment. Douglas's other hand held a cell phone which, in turn, held his attention.

Chase glanced quickly at his reflection in a nearby window to see if he had "sucker" written across his forehead.

He called to the massive kid. "Anthony."

The muscle man kept walking, having not heard Chase over the noise that hammered his eardrums. Chase reached out a hand and touched a chiseled arm as the kid passed. Douglas jerked away, startled.

Chase held his hands up, palms out. "Easy," he said, as if talking to a bear.

"Shit, dawg," Douglas said. "You scared me."

"Sorry. I just—"

"Can't sign no autograph right now." He held up his hand

63

and the snakes danced. "Ain't got time. You know what I'm sayin'?"

Chase feigned disappointment. "That's too bad. Can I ask you a question instead? It won't take long. It's not a math question."

Douglas cocked his head and eyed Chase. He removed the headphones from his ears and hung them around his neck. He knew he had been dissed but wasn't sure how. Probably didn't have enough blood in his brain. It was all feeding oxygen to the massive muscles.

Chase continued before Douglas figured it out and beat him to a pulp with a jug of chocolate milk. "I hear you had a run-in with the campus police recently."

"Huh? Who are you? You a reporter?"

"No, I'm not a reporter. I'm looking for a girl, and I was told you could help me."

Douglas didn't buy it. "I ain't talking to no reporters."

This kid was the poster child for dumb jocks. "Anthony, look," Chase said, "this is important. I'm trying to find a girl who goes to school here. She's missing and might be in danger. Can you help me?"

"I don't know nothin' 'bout no missing girl. You know what I'm sayin'?"

"All I need to know is where you got the drugs that the campus cops found on you?"

"I don't know nothin' 'bout no drugs neither."

Chase sighed, feeling real disappointment this time. "Anthony, I didn't pick you out of a hat. I know the campus cops caught you with drugs. They're the ones who gave me your name."

"They didn't find no drugs, dawg," Douglas insisted. "Just some weed. You know what I'm sayin'?"

"Just some… " Chase sighed, "Okay. Where'd you get the weed?"

"Can't tell you that."

"Come on, kid." Chase was getting frustrated. "Don't make me make you kick my ass. The girl I'm looking for was using. She might have run into some trouble with her dealer. I have to check it out."

Another kid approximately the size of a Brahma bull approached, wiping sweat off his bald head. He stopped next to Douglas and looked Chase up and down. He then looked at Douglas and jerked his head. "Let's jet, dawg."

"Yeah, I be right with you," Douglas told him. To Chase he said, "Look, there's no way this girl did nothin' to nobody. She too little. You know what I'm sayin'?"

It took a second for Chase to absorb what Douglas said. "Wait a minute. The dealer was a girl?"

"Yeah, dawg. But like I said, she too little to do nothin' to nobody."

"Describe her."

Douglas shrugged. The traps pushed his ears up. "I don't know. White girl, about this big." He held the chocolate milk out chest-high. "Blonde hair with like streaks in it."

Chase's gut dropped. "Streaks?"

"Yeah."

"What color?"

"Pink."

Chase sighed. "Shit." He pulled a picture that Sally had printed from Facebook out of his pocket and showed it to Douglas. "That her?"

Douglas took the picture and studied it. He chuckled a little and said, "Yeah, that her." He handed back the photo.

"What are you laughing at?"

"Nothin'," the big man said. "Just that girl. She was crazy. You know what I'm sayin'?"

"Was?"

Douglas nodded. "Haven't seen her in a while. Some dude took her route."

"What? Why didn't you tell me that?"

"I just did."

Chase took a deep breath and let it out through his nose. "You know his name?"

"Naw, man."

"Then how do you find him when you want drugs?"

"I told you, dawg," Douglas said, exasperated. "I don't do drugs."

Chase suppressed a laugh. "I forgot. Weed's not drugs. How do you find this dude when you want weed?"

"I got his cell number."

Laura Phillips happened to be just down the hall from Chase at that very moment, entering the training room. It was a cement-block bunker in the depths of the athletic facility. The florescent lights made the white painted walls brighter than they already were. A giant green thunderbird in midflight adorned the far wall above a dozen bulky, blonde-wood training tables with green-cushioned tops. Two metal whirlpools that looked like deep water troughs sat side by side across the aisle from the training tables. A restaurant-like industrial ice machine hummed in the corner.

It was a place that Laura never wanted to be in during her playing days. A trip to the trainer's room meant you probably wouldn't be playing for a while. The room was empty. The fluorescent lights buzzed. A cocktail of smells of liniments, creams and athletic tape hung heavily in the air. She headed to the small office in the corner. Through the window that overlooked the room, Laura saw the head athletic trainer, Patty Larkin.

They had played soccer together at Michigan. Laura had been a forward, Patty a defender. At five-eleven she had been an intimidating presence for anyone who had made it into the Wolverines' end of the field. They didn't know that Patty was a sweetheart.

"Do these hot tubs work? I could use a soak."

Patty looked up and smiled when she recognized Laura. She wore her dyed platinum-blonde hair in a faux hawk, pushed into a ridge that ran down the center of her head. She stood and exited the small office. "Anything for you, Barbie."

Laura's teammates had called her Barbie, as in Barbie Doll.

The former teammates hugged. Laura almost smothered between Patty's boobs.

Laura stepped back from the embrace. "Did you want me to motorboat those?"

"They're not really big enough for that," Patty said, looking down and pushing her boobs together. "My wife has tried."

"Your wife? My invitation must have gotten lost in the mail."

Patty shrugged sheepishly. "It was a quickie courthouse ceremony. We wanted to get it done before the politicians figured out a way to ban us again. You guys were in Texas, playing the Rangers anyway."

"Well, congratulations. Do I know the lucky bride?"

"No. We met when we played together in Australia."

"An Aussie girl?"

Patty blushed and changed the subject, "What do you want, Barbie?"

"What do you know about Bowe Bradlee?"

"He's tall."

"Can I quote you on that?"

"What do you want to know?"

"I heard he's involved in a missing-girl case. Do you know anything about that?"

"Why would I?"

"Come on, Patty. The trainer's room is like the beauty salon. Anything that's going on with any athlete is talked about."

Patty walked to the door and looked out into the hallway. She came back and lowered her voice. "Off the record?"

"Sure."

"Word is, he was questioned by the police."

"So it's true?"

Patty shrugged. "That's what I hear. Some groupie is missing, and Bowe was questioned. That's all I know."

Chapter 12

O'Ryan's was rocking. For the twenty-somethingth year in a row, the Red Wings had made the playoffs; and every cop who wasn't on duty, and probably a few who were, had crammed in, wearing red and white jerseys and looking pretty much like jackasses as they crowded around the TV above the bar. A few of the guys wore red Styrofoam hats shaped like wingnuts with the word "Wingnut" written across the front. Super jackasses.

Sally wore a Red Wings jersey too. But on her, it looked beyond good. It hung to mid-thigh and the sleeves had been turned back seven or eight times, leaving them just past elbow length. Chase watched her pass out beers like a blackjack dealer until she saw him and scowled.

"Are you just going to stand there? Or are you going to help?"

A collective roar erupted from the crowd. Chase looked at the TV in time to see a Red Wing player celebrating a goal scored.

"A round on the house!" someone yelled, and an even louder cheer went up.

Chase looked at Sally. "What?"

She nodded.

"Whose bright idea was that?"

"Sarge."

Chase joined Sally behind the bar and served up a total of three free rounds. Sarge had thought it would be a good marketing idea to give a round on the house for every goal the Red Wings scored. He might have been right. In the end they sold three times as many as they gave away and sent a platoon of boisterous, drunken cops out into the streets.

It was almost midnight by the time the game ended, the

raucous crowd had dispersed and Sally and Chase had managed to get all the empties stored in the back room. O'Ryan's was still open, but deserted.

They sat at the bar, and Chase told her about his conversation with the tank-like backup defensive tackle.

"So Aley was dealing?"

Chase nodded. "That's what it sounds like."

"That's not good."

"Nope. If she were mixed up in selling drugs, there's no telling what could have happened. She could have come up short with her supplier, or she could have been robbed by a customer and it all went bad."

"Or she could have suffered a hostile takeover," Sally said.

Chase nodded.

"So what are you going to do?"

"I don't know," he admitted. "I guess I'll call her replacement and see if I can set-up a buy. We'll see what happens from there."

"Text," Sally said.

"What?"

"Text him to set-up the buy. Kids don't talk on the phone anymore."

"Really? Why not?"

"Who knows? They're kids. Why did your generation think mullets were cool?"

"*My* generation?"

Sally nodded. "I'm not as old as you, Chase."

They both laughed at that, and then Sally turned serious again.

"It sounds like this young lady got in over her head."

"Yes, it does."

Sally stretched and yawned. "I'm exhausted."

Chase watched and felt a tingle all the way down to his toes. "But you look great."

70

"Shut up!" she said. "I do not. I look like shit."

Chase took her wrist in his left hand and pried her arm away from her face. With his other hand, he pushed her hair back over her left ear. "No. You look great."

They sat like that for a moment while Chase tried to decide what to do next. He wanted to kiss her but didn't know if she would kiss him back or slug him. She preempted his move by jumping off her barstool and wrenching free from his grip.

"I have to go. Can you close up?"

She didn't wait for an answer. She disappeared through the swinging door to the back room before Chase realized what had happened.

"Yeah, I got it," Chase told the swinging door.

He sat by himself in the quiet bar, wondering what was up with Sally. She had started this, hadn't she? Or had Chase misread something? He was so wrapped up in his thoughts that he didn't hear the door open.

"Hey, asshole."

Chase turned to the voice. Andy Clinton stood a few feet away. He wore a navy-blue windbreaker and blue jeans that stopped at mid-gut, making him look like Humpty Dumpty. Why were guys with that build not able to look at themselves in the mirror and see how ridiculous they looked?

"I hear you're butting into my case again," Clinton said.

"You don't have a case. And I'm really not in the mood for your bullshit right now."

Clinton nodded. His face twisted into a maniacal mask with a pained smile and bugged-out eyes. He pointed a stubby finger at Chase. "Stay out of my case. This is your last warning."

Chase got to his feet. "Technically, this is my first warning."

Clinton stepped closer. "First. Last. And only." He poked his finger into Chase's chest with every word.

A Smith & Wesson M&P 40 pistol hung from a shoulder rig under his jacket. Chase didn't think that Sarge would want a gunfight in the middle of O'Ryan's. The insurance on the place was bad enough as it was.

"Go home, Andy," he said.

Clinton continued to nod like a macabre bobblehead. Chase couldn't help wondering what was going through his head. Or was he not thinking at all? What did a dog think about when it growled at another dog?

"You don't have your nigger buddy Warrick here to save your ass this time."

Chase didn't reply. He grabbed the wrist connected to the finger in his chest and spun Clinton, shoving his hand up between his shoulder blades. With the other hand, he reached inside Clinton's jacket and extracted the S&W from the shoulder holster. He dropped it on the ground and moved his hand to the small of Clinton's back, grasped the waistband of his jeans and bum-rushed him to the door. Chase didn't have a hand to open the door with, but didn't care. Clinton slammed face first into the thick slab of wood.

"You might want to open the door," Chase said through clenched teeth.

It had all happened so fast, Clinton hadn't realized what was happening to him. He didn't immediately reach for the door, so Chase pulled him back and shoved his face into it again. Somewhere in the back of his mind, Chase understood that he was basically doing the same thing to Clinton that had been done to him in the Emerson jail. He might regret it at some point, but at the moment it felt damn good to be on this end of the action.

Clinton finally caught on. "You son of a bitch." He grasped the door handle, and the door swung open as Chase pulled him back a second time. This time when Chase shoved they both went through the opened door. Chase took two more steps and then released Clinton with a final shove.

Clinton stumbled a few steps trying to keep his balance, but it had been years since he had been athletic enough to pull off a move like that. He quickly lost the battle with gravity as he stumbled off the curb into the street and went down in a bad parody of a Pete Rose headfirst slide into third base.

"Fuck you!" Chase said, adrenaline surging through his veins like a freight train. "I don't need anyone to save me, and I'll go wherever the hell I want!"

Chapter 13

Chase was amped up from the confrontation with Clinton and knew he wouldn't be able to sleep. He sent a text to Anthony Douglas's weed supplier and then waited what seemed like an eternity for a reply. He was careful not to be too specific about the drugs. The dealer probably wouldn't respond to a text that could ultimately incriminate him. At least Chase hoped the kid wasn't that dumb.

His phone rang a few minutes later. Chase recognized the number on the caller ID as the one he had sent the text to. He punched the answer button. "Hello."

"Who is this?" the caller asked. His voice was male and white. They had replaced the white girl with a white guy. Chase didn't know why, but it was an interesting fact. Why would they be using white kids? He'd bet anything that the suppliers were black.

"I'm a friend of Anthony Douglas. He said you could hook me up."

There was a pause. "If you really were a friend of Anthony's, you wouldn't have texted. He knows I'm not dumb enough to put anything in writing.

Chase suppressed a laugh. Sally had called that one wrong. "Yeah, sorry," he said into the phone. "My bad."

The dealer paused longer this time. Probably trying to decide if he were being set up. Eventually he said, "You know The Bird's Nest?"

"Yeah, sure."

"I'll be here another hour or so."

Chase told him he'd see him soon, but he was talking to himself. The kid had already hung up.

He locked up O'Ryan's and headed up Woodward, back to D State. Plenty of people still milled around the campus.

Cold, Dark Places

When Chase was a kid, his mom had told him nothing good ever happened after midnight. Like that was supposed to make him want to stay home. Hell, telling a teenager that nothing good was going on out there only made them want to be out there even more. What fun was it to go home before the bad stuff started?

The Bird's Nest was mostly full. Music blared. A low rumble of conversation was pierced periodically by screams of laughter and boys egging each other on to chug a beer or other stupid macho shit that college boys do to show off for girls. Everybody was drinking, though most of the clientele didn't look old enough. Chase maneuvered his way through the crowd to the bar and ordered a beer. The bartender brought a bottle of Budweiser and gave it to him, along with a you're-too-old-to-be-here look. He returned the look with a mind-your-own-business look and turned his back to the bar.

The place wasn't exactly a sports bar, but it was painted in the school's colors. A pretty cool mural of a giant black bird in mid-flight, emerging from a bank of slate-gray storm clouds with lightening connecting its wings to the clouds, took up an entire wall. Sports memorabilia and pictures adorned the other walls like one of those franchise casual-dining restaurants. One kid sat alone in a booth. He was the only one in the bar, other than Chase, not engaged in conversation. His fingers worked feverishly at the buttons of a cell phone. A backpack sat on the bench seat between him and the wall. Now why would this kid have a backpack in a bar at 1 a.m.? He either had drugs in it or guns. In this day and age, it was about as likely that he had guns in there and was working up the courage to shoot the place up.

Chase walked to the booth and slide in across from the kid. The kid looked up from the phone and raised his eyebrows in confusion. He was far from what one would perceive to be a drug dealer, which might be just what the suppliers were looking for in a dealer. He definitely wouldn't bring any suspicion onto himself. He was a skinny little white guy, clean-shaven with round glasses that slid down his nose. The hostile-takeover theory was out the window.

He pushed the glasses up and said, "Can I help you?"

Chase looked over both shoulders and then back to him. "You the guy?" he said, even though he recognized the voice.

"What guy?"

"You know…" he sucked at pinched fingers in the international symbol of smoking a joint.

The kid laughed. "You did *not* just do that."

"What?"

The kid shook his head. "Aren't you a little old to be in here?"

"Is there an age limit?"

"No, I guess not," the kid said, reaching for the backpack. "What are you looking for?"

"Just like that?"

"Just like what?"

"You're not very good at this, are you? How do you know I'm not a cop?"

The kid shrugged. "I don't know. Why do you have to be a cop? Maybe you have like glaucoma or something."

"Glaucoma?"

The kid shrugged his shoulders again. "It's the only old-people disease I could think of."

Chase resisted the urge to hit the whippersnapper. "What I'm looking for is information."

Now the kid was really confused. "Information about what?"

"Who you're working for. I need the name of your supplier."

"My supplier? Are you a cop?"

"Now you ask? A minute ago you were ready to sell me drugs, and you didn't care if I were a cop."

"Yeah, well, a minute ago you weren't asking about my supplier. I'd rather sell drugs to a cop than tell you who I work for."

"That bad?"

"You have no idea."

It was the exact same reaction that Slick Rick had had at the strip club. "How'd you get into this mess in the first place?"

The kid shrugged. It seemed to be his go-to move. "I screwed up. I bought on credit and didn't have the money when they came to collect. They told me I could work off the debt if I became their new salesman here on campus, and they wouldn't put a beat down on me. How could I say 'no' to an offer like that?"

"What happened to their old salesman?"

"I don't know. I don't know anything about any of this. A kid in my dorm told me that speed would help me stay up for all-night study sessions. I have a double major and I'm trying to study for the MCATs on top of that. It's killing me."

"Next time try a 5-Hour Energy."

"I know, right?" the kid said with an ironic laugh. Then he shook his head. "It's a little late now."

Chase looked around the bar to make sure nobody was paying any attention to them. They weren't. He turned back to the kid. "I'll tell you what, you get me a meeting with your supplier and I'll help you get out from under all this."

"Really? How?"

"Let me worry about that," he said and started to slide out of the booth. "What's your name, anyway?"

"Tim."

"Okay, Doctor Tim. I'll be in touch. Try to stay out of trouble until then."

Chapter 14

Chase didn't make it down to O'Ryan's the next day until almost 10 a.m. He hadn't gotten to bed until after 3 a.m., and he was a little tired and crabby. He had missed the morning rush... again. Sarge didn't say anything when Chase walked in, which was unusual. He had expected some kind of smart-ass comment about his being late. Instead, Sarge concentrated on his crossword puzzle and ignored Chase.

Mo Warrick exited the bathroom as Chase poured himself a cup of coffee. "You working part-time now?" Warrick said. "Leaving Sarge to do all the heavy lifting in the morning?"

Chase looked at Sarge. Was he sulking? He wanted Sarge to call him Denzel or asshole or something. He held the mug up to his lips and blew into it and then took a sip of the coffee. "I got in late last night."

"I heard you had some excitement here last night."

"Red Wings game and Sarge's brilliant marketing idea." Chase hoped it would perk Sarge up, but he acted as if he hadn't heard.

Warrick shook his head. "Nope, not the Red Wings."

Chase cocked his head. "What are you talking about, Mo?"

"Clinton."

"Oh." He laughed. After his trip to The Bird's Nest, he had forgotten about Clinton. "That dumb-ass."

Warrick nodded. "That dumb-ass is pressing charges."

"He's what?"

"He says you assaulted him."

"I threw him out of my bar. I believe I have the right to do that."

"Not by assaulting him."

78

Chase laughed again. This had to be a joke. "Come on, Mo. You've got to be joking."

Warrick shook his head. "Wish I were, Chase. Off the record, I'm jealous as hell that I didn't get to ram his face into a door, but I'm not joking. He swore out a complaint. I just wanted to give you a head's-up."

"What a piece of shit," Chase said, disgusted.

"Yeah," Warrick said. "Anyway, where you at with the missing girl?"

Chase refilled Warrick's coffee cup and then walked around the bar. They sat side by side with their cups of coffee and discussed a nineteen-year-old girl, missing in one of the most dangerous cities in the world like a couple of guys discussing the weather.

"It's not looking too good for the girl," Chase said. "I hope to hell she *did* pack a bag and make a run for it. Otherwise she's in a world of shit." He went on to tell Warrick about the football player—without mentioning his name—and the fact that Aley was his dealer. He then described the conversation with her replacement, Dr. Tim and how scared the kid and Slick Rick were of the BD Boyz.

"So you think it's the BD Boyz?" Warrick said.

Chase shrugged. "That would be my guess. If she were selling on credit and didn't have the money when her supplier came to collect.... "

Warrick whistled softly. "Lord have mercy. What has this young lady gotten herself mixed up in?"

Just then Chase's cell phone vibrated in his pocket. He pulled it out and saw that he had a text message. He opened the message. It was from Dr. Tim and said, "He wants to meet tonight."

"I think I'm going to find out tonight," Chase told Warrick.

Trudy DeRosa laughed. "Sergeant Clinton? He's a

worthless piece of shit."

"No, don't hold back," Laura Phillips said. "Tell me how you really feel."

Trudy laughed again. Her laugh was sultry and smooth, as if she practiced it hours a day. It fit her well. She was a classic beauty, the kind that made men weak in the knees and women jealous and hate her for no other reason than that she was so beautiful. And like many beautiful women, she didn't even know it. She didn't try to be beautiful, she just was, and didn't care. Laura wanted to hate her, but Trudy was something of a mentor to her.

They had met at a Detroit Press Club event. Somehow, as always seems to happen, the two most beautiful people in the room gravitated to each other. They had struck up an immediate friendship, though Trudy was a good ten years older than Laura. Having been around the block a time or two, Trudy took the younger woman under her wing. Even though they worked in different medias, they were both journalists and both understood the glass ceiling that came with their looks and gender. Beauty for a woman might open doors, but it also makes the men in what was still a very male-dominated profession not take them seriously.

Trudy had gotten the scoop on the Woodstock baby story the year before. It was a big story, a forty-year-old mystery solved. It wasn't Watergate or the Pentagon Papers, but it had gotten her a book deal. She had taken a sabbatical from her job on the newspaper to write it.

They were sitting at a table in a deli in the Eastern Market. The lunch rush was at a standstill as the young countermen stared at the two beautiful women. Neither noticed, having dealt with it their entire lives.

Trudy placed the turkey club she was eating on her plate and leaned closer. "Was there something you didn't understand?"

"No, I understood. I'm just not sure how it helps me."

"If you're looking for help, don't look to Clinton."

"So where do I look?"

Trudy picked up the sandwich and took another bite. She thought while she chewed. "Let me make a couple calls."

Chapter 15

He stood in the darkened doorway of a convenience store that had been closed for at least two decades. The bulb in the streetlight overhead had burned out sometime before that and never been replaced. The glass in the window frames and door had long since been smashed out, and plywood covered with about fifteen layers of graffiti filled the openings. Doctor Tim stood on the corner across the street under the only working streetlight in the neighborhood. Chase could see his body shaking. The shivers probably weren't from the weather. It was cold, but not that cold.

An old beater Oldsmobile with tinted back windows eased to the curb not three feet from where Chase hid in the darkened doorway. He reached inside his coat and grasped the handle of the Beretta in the holster on his hip. Tim stepped off the curb and crossed the street. The driver rolled down his window and flicked a cigarette butt. The lights from the dashboard lit up his face. He was black, in his early twenties. The thick, gold rope around his neck probably cost more than the car. Another kid rode shotgun. There wasn't enough light in the car to make out his features, and the tinted windows made it impossible to see if anybody sat in the back seat. Chase had no idea if it were just the two of them or if there were an entire platoon in the car.

He waited for Tim to reach the Olds before stepping out of the doorway. The passenger had his head turned, watching Tim along with the driver. It was a lucky break for Chase. The purpose of the shotgun rider was to protect the driver. That meant watching for trouble, not looking at the same thing as the driver. If Chase's luck held, the door would be unlocked and the backseat would be empty. Tim reached the car.

"You got my money?" the driver said. His voice was high and intense, in a wired-too-tight kind of way.

Tim handed a small roll of cash through the window. Chase stepped from the doorway and pulled the Beretta from the holster with his left hand and grasped the passenger door handle with his right. It wasn't ideal, but that's what the situation warranted since he was on the passenger side. He was pretty sure the backseat was empty, but not one hundred percent. He wouldn't be able to control the situation if there were armed gangsters in the back seat to deal with, along with the two in the front, so a sneak attack was the best approach. He didn't want his tombstone to read "He's dead because he played fair." Well, actually that wouldn't be a bad epitaph. It was the thought of the tombstone in general that bothered him.

Chase yanked the door open and swung the Beretta backhanded into the passenger's head all in one fluid motion. It caught the gangbanger high on the cheekbone just below the temple. His chin hit his chest and he slumped forward. Chase transferred the gun to his right hand and pointed it at the driver's head.

"Get out of the car!"

Tim ran off, just as Chase had told him to do. Chase looked quickly into the back seat. It was empty, obviously. If it hadn't been, he would have been dead by then. The driver reached for a beat-to-hell revolver between his legs, and Chase shot the window out next to his head.

"Fuck!" the kid said, dropping the gun. It disappeared into blackness by the gangbanger's feet.

Chase took a second to get his breathing under control. It doesn't matter how many times someone has been in a life-or-death situation, the adrenaline always goes crazy when the shit hits the fan. He said, "Get out of the car... " with as much calm as he could muster "...and leave the gun."

The driver pushed open the door and started to climb out. Chase hit the passenger once more with the Beretta to make sure he stayed put. This time he used his right hand and hit him in the back of the head.

"Keep your hands where I can see them."

The driver stood with his hands up and looked at Chase over the roof of the car. He wore a white, wife-beater tee-shirt and a black bandana around his head with the knot in the front, Tupac-style.

"Hey, man," he said, "you can't be bustin' my dawg in the face and blowin' out my fuckin' window. There rules 'bout that kinda' shit."

Chase pointed the gun right between his eyes. "You don't play by the rules; why should I?"

"You 5-0. You *have* to play by the rules."

"I'm not a cop."

It took a second to register, and then the kid realized he was up a creek.

Chase nodded his head. "Yeah," he said in confirmation.

The kid manned up. In the face of his own death, he didn't whine or cry or beg for his life. He sneered and said, "Fuck it. You gonna do it, do it."

"I'm not going to kill you," Chase said, "if you give me the answers I want."

"What answers?"

"Where's Aley Beach?"

"Who?"

Chase squeezed off a shot. It zinged past the banger's ear and blew off a small chunk of the corner of the building across the street.

"Wrong answer."

"Shit!" the kid said. "You crazy? You know who I am?"

Chase nodded. "Sure. You're a scumbag drug dealer."

"I BD!"

"That supposed to mean something to me?" Chase said. "BD Boyz die just like everybody else. Now, where's Aley Beach?"

The kid looked down the barrel of the Beretta for a moment and then said, "I don't know where that bitch at."

"I don't believe you."

"I don't give a fuck you don't believe me. That for reals. I. Don't. Know. You think I *want that* fuckin' Herb grinding for me? Shit. That shorty Aley was dope. She down with the jocks."

He had a point. But— "I heard she sold on credit. That's how you got Tim."

"Fuck that. She good for it. If not, she can work it off another way." He grinned at that, and Chase seriously wanted to shoot him.

"When's the last time you saw her?"

"Two, three weeks."

"She owe you money?"

"Not enough to kill her."

"Kill her? What makes you think she's dead?"

"Shit," the kid said, drawing it out about four beats. "You think a little white girl like that go missin' in this town and she still alive? You a dumb motherfucker you think that."

Chase almost believed him, even though he knew better than to believe anything a gangbanger said. But he really didn't think the kid knew anything about Aley Beach's disappearance.

"What's your name?"

"Why you axing?"

"Because I want to know."

"Fuck you."

Chase sighed. "Are you really going to make me shoot you over your name?"

The gangbanger thought for a second, probably trying to figure out why Chase wanted to know. Chase was really just curious. He finally said, "G Money."

"That the name your mama gave you?"

"What the fuck, Holmes?" G Money said, genuinely confused.

Chase waved the Beretta at him. He was just messing with the kid at that point. "Come on. What'd your mama name you?"

"Gerald, a'rite? My name is Gerald."

"Last name?"

Gerald hesitated. Chase tapped the Beretta on the roof of the Olds.

"Robinson!" Gerald said. "Gerald Robinson! Motherfucker!"

Chase nodded his head, feeling better that he had gotten something out of the conversation. "All right, Gerald," he said, and saw the banger's jaw clench. "There's just one more thing. Tim is out."

"Yeah, he out a'rite. I'ma bust a cap in his ass. Snitch motherfucker drop a dime on me."

Chase circled the car, keeping the Beretta aimed between G Money's eyes. "He dropped a dime because I said I'd get him out."

"I jus' tol' you—"

Chase shoved the barrel of the gun into Gerald's forehead midway between the top of his nose and the knot of the bandana. He shoved, bending the kid backwards onto the roof of the car. "He's out," Chase said slow and quiet. "You *will not* bust a cap in his ass; you *will not* contact him; you *will not* go anywhere near him."

Gerald glared at Chase, probably trying to decide if he'd really shoot him in cold blood. "A'rite! Shit!" he finally said.

"Give me your word."

"What?"

"Give me your word."

"My word? What kinda white boy bullshit is that?"

Chase pushed a little harder with the gun. "Do it."

"A'rite! Fuck it. He out."

Chase nodded. "Remember, Gerald," he said, "I found you once, I can find you again. I find out you even think about Tim after this, and I *will* kill you."

Chase pulled the gun back and Gerald straightened. He had a circle indented in his forehead from the gun barrel.

"Now get back in the car, and get out of here before you catch pneumonia."

Gerald's eyes flicked to the gun that lay on the driver's seat.

"You touch that gun, I'll bust a cap in *your* ass," Chase said. "Understand?"

Gerald nodded and dropped his hands. "Watch your back, dawg," he said, ducking into the driver's seat. He dropped the beater into gear and drove off with a squawk of tires and a cloud of exhaust fumes.

O'Ryan's was mostly empty when he got back. One guy sat at the bar watching the TV, and two guys sat at a table near the door bullshitting each other about how many perps they'd shot.

"Hey, Denzel," one of the guys at the table called as Chase entered.

Chase flipped them the bird without looking to see who had said it. Both guys laughed. Some things never get old.

Sally had already started cleaning up for the night. Chase walked around the bar and helped her load empty bottles into the empty cases. She didn't acknowledge him. He wasn't doing too well lately with his partners.

He waded in anyway. "We have a good night?"

Sally shrugged. "Tigers game on TV. So the normal baseball crowd, along with the usual drunks." She looked at the two guys at the table.

Chase took hold of her shoulders and turned her to face him. "What's going on?"

She looked at him with those green eyes that he loved. "I don't know," she said.

"Did I misread something? I thought that you were flirting with me. Now I feel like a creeper, trying to force myself on you."

"No, I was. I'm sorry. It's not you. Well, it is you. But it's me too."

Chase shook his head. "What?"

"I mean... I do want to, but... I'm scared. Okay?"

"Of me?"

"Not of you, exactly. You know my husband died in the line of duty. I promised myself I'd never get involved with another cop and have that happen again. Now I have feelings for you, and you're *not* a cop; but you still have people threatening to shoot you, knocking you around in jail cells and god knows what else. I can't go through that again, Chase. I can't lose somebody else the way I lost Chris."

They had never talked about it, but the death of Sally's husband had been national news. He had been a patrolman, only on the job for a few years when he pulled over a car on a routine traffic stop. The driver of the car pulled a gun and shot him dead on the side of the road. It happened so fast that the poor guy hadn't even drawn his own gun. The dash cam in his patrol car recorded the whole thing and had been shown ad nauseam on the cable news channels. The video never showed the driver, who shot from inside the car, and the car the perp was driving had been reported stolen, so they hadn't been able to trace the killer that way either. Unfortunately for Chris, the stolen car report hadn't been broadcast by the time he had pulled it over. If it had been, he would have been warned. The case went cold sometime soon after the cable news sharks had moved onto the next sensational story and was still open and unsolved.

Chase let go of Sally's shoulders. "I get it." He was disappointed, but what kind of a relationship can you have with someone if she's scared all the time that you're going to die?

"I'm sorry," Sally said.

"It's okay. I understand."

Sally disappeared through the swinging door to the back

room. Chase watched her until the door stopped swinging, and then he turned and scanned the room. A woman sat in one of the booths in the back. He hadn't noticed her while his attention had been occupied with Sally. In the dim light, he saw blonde hair and calves protruding from a knee-length skirt.

Who is that? He was sure that she wasn't a regular, but she looked familiar. He stared for a couple of beats longer, and then it hit him. She did the Tigers games on TV... like a sideline reporter. He wandered across the room to introduce himself. She looked up at his approach. Her beauty was almost too much to look at, like looking at the sun.

She took his offered hand. "It's nice to meet you, Mr. Chase. Laura Phillips. Word on the street is you're looking into the Bowe Bradlee case."

Chase didn't want to give back the hand. It was smooth and cool and fit perfectly into his hand. He was so taken by her beauty that he didn't process what she had said. He saw her mouth move, but the words didn't register. It wasn't until she pulled her hand out of his grip and gave him the did-you-hear-what-I-said look that he realized he was standing there like a boob staring at the sun.

"Um," he said, because he really hadn't heard what she had said and didn't know what to say.

"Bowe Bradlee?"

"Bowe... oh, right. Bowe. What about him?"

"You're looking into his case?"

"Oh, right. It's not really Bowe's case, though. I'm looking for a missing girl. Bowe's name just happened to come up in the case."

The light in Laura Phillips' eyes faded. "Oh, so he's not a suspect."

"Like, officially? I don't know. I'm not official. I'm just a guy looking for a girl."

"But I hear Bowe's high school coach asked you to find him."

The fact that he was talking to a reporter and not just a beautiful woman finally hit Chase. "Where'd you hear that?"

"Around."

"Around? Really? Who I talk to just happens to be common knowledge on the streets?"

"So Ty Jackson *did* ask you to find Bowe Bradlee."

"Find Bowe Bradlee? Now I'm looking for Bowe Bradlee?"

"So you are looking for Bowe."

Chase shook his head and turned to leave. "I think I've said enough."

"Wait, please."

He stopped but didn't turn back.

"Look, I understand you don't want to talk to me. But I need your help."

Chase turned back to the beautiful woman. "Need *my* help? It sounds like you already know everything I know."

Laura Phillips sighed. "I'm stuck here, Mr. Chase. I was all-state in three sports in high school, I went to the University of Michigan and graduated *magna cum laude* while playing varsity soccer all four years. I've got the talent, the looks and the background to be big, but I can't catch a fucking break. I should be doing a national show, but I'm stuck in Detroit doing this sideline bullshit on a regional broadcast."

"Detroit's not so bad."

She looked at him like he was an idiot. It was a look he'd seen before.

"If I can break this Bowe Bradlee thing, I can go big time and get out of this hell hole."

Chase was a bit hurt by her portrayal of his hometown. "I understand what you're saying, but I really can't help you."

"I think you can. I think you know more than you're letting on."

"I wish."

Chapter 16

He drank a few beers with the drunks and then a few more by himself after they left. Then he climbed the stairs to the apartment he lived in above O'Ryan's. It wasn't much, but it came with the bar and Chase lived there for free if you didn't count the money he had poured into the bar to begin with.

After what seemed like ten minutes, he awoke to the sound of his cell phone ringing. He was sprawled on the old leather couch. Apparently, he hadn't made it to the bed. It was still dark out. He fumbled the phone open and said, "What?"

"You're going to want to see this," a voice rumbled.

It took Chase a second to recognize Mo Warrick's voice and half a second longer to be wide awake.

"See what?" he said, sitting up on the couch.

"Just get down here."

"Where?"

"Alfred, between John R and Brush."

Alfred is just a few blocks north of both Comerica Park and Ford Field, the home field of the Lions. As pretty much the entire block was empty, it was a popular place for people attending games to park and tailgate. There weren't any tailgate parties going on when Chase arrived, though. There were, however, several police cars with their red and blue roof lights twirling. Two cars at each end of the block restricted access to the crime scene.

Chase parked on John R in almost the exact same place as he had when he had gone to the Tigers game. He was pretty sure what he would find when he got out of the car. He shook his head at the thought that he had been that close to

Aley Beach and didn't even know it.

The cops from the patrol cars that blocked the street were arguing with a someone in a black wool trench coat with the hood up. Her back was to Chase, but he had a pretty good idea who it was.

"Please return to your car and move along," the senior of the two said to her.

The younger cop looked at Chase as he crossed the street. "Warrick," Chase said. The cop nodded him past the barricade.

He had almost made it past the roadblock when Laura Phillips said, "Chase!"

"Shit," he said to himself and stopped. He turned and she hit him with the most pathetic, pleading look he had ever seen. He knew he was going to regret it, but heard himself say, "She's with me."

The cops almost looked relieved. She was now his problem; they had plausible deniability. "He said she was with him. How did we know we weren't supposed to let her past?"

Chase and the reporter walked toward a cluster of cops standing in a circle near a dead tree. Chase wondered if the dead tree were symbolic or just a messed up-coincidence. Weeds rose knee-high and whisked at their legs. An unmistakable stench floated on the wind.

"Oh my god," Laura Phillips said. "What's that smell?"

"Death."

She buried her mouth and nose down inside the wool coat. In a muffled voice she said, "Good Lord."

"How'd you find out about this?" Chase said.

"Police scanner. Dead bodies have been popping up all over the city. This was the first Caucasian female."

They approached the huddle. The cops, including Clinton and Warrick, looked down at the body of a young woman. She was on her front, her face turned to the right. In profile

Chase recognized the young lady he had been so desperately searching for, Aley Beach. She wore the same black miniskirt and white blouse that she had been reported to be wearing when she disappeared. Her right leg was bent in a running pose, but she hadn't been running. It was simply how she had ended up when dumped.

Chase didn't have to ask how she had been found. He'd seen it too many times. The warm weather that he had enjoyed while watching the Tigers play just a few blocks away had thawed her enough to get decomposition started. Someone had either found the body themselves or simply called 911 and reported the stench.

Chase looked at Clinton. He had two black eyes, which Chase would have enjoyed the hell out of if there hadn't been a dead girl at their feet. "Would this be further developments?" he said.

"Fuck you, Chase!" Clinton said. He reached across the huddle and shoved him. His fat hands hit Chase's chest with the force of a donkey kick, which would have been ironic, coming from a jackass, if, again, there hadn't been a dead girl lying at their feet. "She's probably been dead the whole time."

Much to his dismay, Chase staggered back a step. He caught his balance and then launched himself at Clinton. He grabbed him by the lapels of his cheap Sears suit. "You lazy son of a bitch! If I find out she was lying in this field dying while you were sitting on your fat ass—"

"Enough!" Warrick said. He grabbed the back of Chase's jacket at the neck. Very quietly he said, "Let him go" into Chase's ear.

Chase let go, and Warrick walked him away from the huddle by the scruff of his neck.

"You know he's right," Warrick said.

"I know," Chase said. He was pissed. He had known the whole time that she had probably been dead, but he had held out hope that she'd be found alive. "Dammit!"

A coroner's van pulled to a stop at the curb on Alfred. The passenger side door opened, and a slightly-built Asian man hopped to the pavement. "Son of a bitch," he said. "Why can't they ever dump them next to the road? Why does it always have to be way on the other side of the fucking lot?"

Chase chuckled and shook his head in spite of the horror of the moment and the anger he felt at it.

"Tommy Chin," Warrick said.

"Gotta love him," Chase replied.

"No, I don't."

Tommy kicked through the weeds while an assistant, the driver, pulled a gurney out of the back of the van. It had probably been a long night for Tommy, and he was definitely showing the strain. "Glad to see everybody hard at work," he said as he neared.

"Hey, Tommy," Warrick said as he and Chase returned to the huddle, "I don't want to listen to your bullshit. Shut the fuck up and do your job!"

They all watched while Tommy did his thing.

"How long has she been here?" Clinton asked.

"She's thawing on the outside but still pretty cold near the core," Tommy said. "She's been here a while. I'll try to nail it down when we get her back to the morgue."

"Cause of death?" Clinton said.

"I'll make it official when I get her on the table, but what I'm seeing here is consistent with strangulation."

"Wouldn't there be a more pronounced line around the neck from the ligature?"

"Manual strangulation," Tommy said. "Someone squeezed the life out of this girl with his bare hands."

Laura stood quietly, her mouth and nose buried in the collar of her coat, which was doing a horrible job of filtering the stench. The police officers and medical responders did their thing all around her. Like most people, she had never seen a dead body outside of a funeral home. Everybody has seen a dead body in a casket at a funeral home, but it's not the same. In the funeral home, the mortician has cleaned up the body, dressed it nicely, applied makeup and, in some cases, even cut and styled the dead person's hair. The body lies there looking as if they are napping and will wake at any minute. This was very, very different. The poor girl's stark-white skin hung slack from her arms and legs. Her face was twisted in a mask of horror; her eyes and mouth both wide open. She had died a horrible, terrifying death. Laura fought back tears, thinking of this poor girl dying alone in this cold dark place.

She couldn't peel her eyes off of the body. She watched every moment of the medical examiner's work until the body bag's zipper closed over the macabre expression.

The huddle broke up as the gurney carrying the body was wheeled away. Chase led the pack, almost running to get away. The anger he had expressed had been palpable. The woman in her wanted to follow him, to ease his pain. The reporter in her, the one who had led her to an empty lot in Detroit in the middle of the night in search of the story that would make her career, went the other way.

"Detective," she called to Clinton's back.

He stopped and turned to face her. The sun was cresting the horizon, backlighting him. His eyes roamed from her toes to the top of her head, making her feel like a specimen under a microscope. "You're Chase's friend."

Laura sensed the hate in the detective's voice. "I wouldn't say 'friend.'"

"He brought you."

"We met here."

Clinton huffed. "What do you want?"

"I want to know what happened. Who did this to her."

"You working with Chase to get the nig—African-American off?"

Laura didn't miss the near *faux pas*. She didn't react to it, but noted it and filed it away. "Which African-American are you referring to? Bowe Bradlee?"

Clinton looked at her again. This time he was really looking at her, not just trying to see through her clothes. "Who are you anyway?"

Laura told him.

"A reporter?" Clinton said with a laugh. "Chase brought a reporter to a crime scene?"

Laura decided to play into Clinton's obvious bias. "Look, detective, I'm going to level with you. I know Aley Beach was with Bradlee the night she went missing."

"You do?"

"I do. I also know that Bradlee is a… how do you say it... person of interest?"

Clinton paused for a moment, trying to decide if he could use this reporter to his benefit. It couldn't hurt, so he said, "You can't use my name, but I can confirm for you that we are looking for Bradlee. We'd like to have another talk with him."

"So he's a suspect?"

Clinton looked over his shoulder and then back to Laura. "I didn't say that. I think at this point, 'person of interest' would be more accurate."

She watched him walk away, trying not to jump up and down and scream like a school girl. There was a story here, a big one, one that could catapult her into the big time.

She watched the crime-scene unit work the lot. They picked through the weeds, picking up every piece of trash, bagging it and cataloging it. It would take all day to get it all. Afterwards it would be the cleanest empty lot in the city.

The contacts page of her cell phone stared up at her. The contact's name was Brad Hamilton. He was an associate producer on a national NBA show. Laura had met him when the show was in town doing a piece on Bowe for the upcoming draft coverage. She hadn't had anything to do with the taping but had hung around trying to make some connections with the national guys. Brad had given her his number, but she was hesitant to call him. If the pig found out that she had gone around him, he would throw a shit fit. She didn't really care; she just didn't know if her career could survive being fired. Lots of on-air personalities had been fired, but only the big stars got second chances.

She finally took a deep breath and pushed the call button, like she was pushing the launch button on a nuclear weapon. If this didn't go right, it would have the same affect.

Brad answered after five rings. Laura had almost disconnected after every one. He sounded as if she had woken him, and then she remembered that he was in Los Angeles, three hours behind Detroit. It was like 4 a.m. there.

"Hi, Brad," she said into the phone. "I'm so sorry I woke you. This is Laura Phillips in Detroit. We met when—"

He cut her off. "Laura. Yeah, I remember. How are you?"

"I'm good. You?"

"Can't complain, you know, except for it being the middle of the night."

Laura cringed. "I'm so sorry. I forgot you were in LA."

"It's all right," he said. "We're crazy busy with the draft coming up and all, I haven't been asleep very long anyway."

Decision time. She could still not do this. She could say she was just calling to say hi or something lame like that. Then she flashed on her dad and something he told her once. He had said, "Sometimes you just have to say fuck it and jump." Her dad had never steered her wrong, so she took another deep breath and jumped.

"That's what I'm calling you about," she said, "the draft."

"Oh?" He had that non-committal tone in his voice that

said he had people calling him all the time with shit they thought was good but failed to make the cut.

"Yes. I think I have something here."

Brad sighed into the phone. "Listen, Laura—"

"It's about Bowe Bradlee."

Silence came from the phone and then, "What about Bowe Bradlee?"

"I'm not sure exactly, but he's mixed up in something here. Something big."

"How big?" The weariness in his voice had changed to interest.

"Earthshattering."

"Really?"

"It's my story, Brad," Laura said. "If you want it, it comes from me. We're a package deal."

Chapter 17

The sun had risen by the time Chase made it back to his apartment. It was going to be another beautiful day. He thought briefly about Sarge down in O'Ryan's. He should go down and help with the morning rush, but the thought left his head as soon as it hit the pillow. He slept for another couple of hours until his cell phone woke him again. He flipped it open and answered without bothering to see who it was.

"Turn on the TV," Mo Warrick said.

Chase didn't question him. He got up and turned the TV on. Laura Phillips came on the screen, standing in knee-high weeds. The dead tree from the empty lot where Aley Beach's body had been found was framed over her left shoulder. "Shit."

"The young lady had been missing for almost a month before being found early this morning. Preliminary reports show manual strangulation as the cause of death. It is very early in the investigation, but police are searching for Detroit State University power forward Bowe Bradlee."

The screen split; the anchor in the studio appeared on the left side. He was a male version of Laura Phillips. "Has Bradlee been named a suspect?"

Laura Phillips filled the right side of the screen. "Not at this time, although police have witnesses linking Bradlee to the victim on the night she disappeared and would very much like to talk with him."

"I knew I was going to regret it," Chase said to the TV.

He showered and put on clean clothes, then headed down the metal stairs mounted to the side of the building. The one gripe Chase had about the apartment was that there weren't interior stairs that connected it with O'Ryan's. It would have been nice not to have to go outside during the cold months. It also would have been nice not to have to go outside when gigantic thugs were waiting on the sidewalk in front of the building.

The thug in question that day was at least six-seven and could have played offensive tackle for the Lions. In fact, Chase thought as he studied the behemoth, he looked like a guy who *had* played offensive tackle for the Lions a few years before; but he couldn't put a name with the face. He was black and wore faded black jeans that normal people could have used as a sleeping bag and a thigh-length, black leather coat.

"Get in the car," the thug said, indicating a shiny black Cadillac Escalade parked at the curb.

Chase smiled, trying to be as non-confrontational as possible. "Actually, I don't need a ride. I'm just headed into this here bar."

The thug pulled an all-black semi-auto pistol out of his coat pocket like a magician. It went nicely with his outfit. Of course, black goes with everything.

"I ain't asking."

"Did I mention it's a cop bar?"

The big man pointed the gun at Chase. "Get in the fucking car."

"All right, all right," Chase said, raising his hands. "Don't get your panties in a bunch. Hey, by the way, did you play for the Lions?"

The thug pulled open the rear door of the Escalade with the hand that held the gun and shoved Chase in with the other. Chase managed to duck in time to not hit his head on the roof.

He landed on a black leather seat that was, without a doubt, made of the softest leather he had ever sat on. He sank into it and only then realized that he sat next to another black man. This one was a little older, evidenced by the sprinkling of gray in his afro and beard. He wore all black as well: black suit, black shirt, black tie.

"Don't give Kendrick a hard time," the man said. "It takes forever to get him calmed down again."

Chase snapped his fingers. "Kendrick Martin." He *had* played offensive tackle for the Lions. He had been a backup and had only started a few games, filling in when the starters were hurt; but he had hung on the roster for a few years. Chase was a little disappointed to learn where Kendrick had ended up after football, and then it hit him. "And you're Howard Frazier."

Frazier was a sports agent with a rather notorious reputation. He represented only black players and was not above playing the race card when it suited his needs.

A small smile creased his face, pleased that Chase had recognized him.

"Can you get me Kendrick's autograph?"

The smile disappeared. "I hear you're looking into the disappearance of the girl from D State."

"Murder."

"What?"

"Don't you watch TV? She's not missing anymore. She was found this morning, dead."

Frazier sighed. He wanted to yell and curse, but he kept his cool. In his business, it was counter-productive to show emotion. He simply said, "I see. Was Bowe Bradlee mentioned in the news report?"

"What's it to you?" Chase asked.

"Bowe Bradlee is one of my boys. So I'm interested."

"One of your boys?"

"One of my clients."

"Isn't he still in college?"

Frazier scoffed. "Don't be naïve. I've owned that boy since he was in the eighth grade."

"Oh," Chase said, "I see."

Frazier nodded. "I have a lot invested in that kid. *A lot.* I intend to see that investment pay off. And that means he goes number one in the draft."

"Okay, but what's that got to do with me?"

"It's not going to happen if he has a cloud hanging over him. You remember that football player from LSU? He was a sure bet for the first round until his name came up in a murder investigation. The fact that he was innocent didn't matter. Nobody would touch him."

Chase did remember. La'el Collins had been a sure-shot first-round pick in the NFL draft. Three days before the draft, a pregnant ex-girlfriend of his had been murdered. It was revealed that the police in Baton Rouge wanted to talk to Collins in connection with the murder. Even though they did not say he was a suspect, Collins went from the first round to undrafted. It was later revealed that the baby the woman had been carrying was not his, and Collins had had nothing to do with the murder. But it was too little too late; the damage had been done.

"Didn't he sign with the Cowboys after the police cleared him?" Chase said.

Frazier scoffed. "As an undrafted free agent. Do you have any idea the difference in money between a first-round pick and an undrafted free agent?"

Chase shrugged. "A lot?"

"Damn straight. So, was Bowe mentioned in the report?"

"He was. He was called a person of interest."

Frazier pinched the bridge of his nose, squeezed his eyes shut and forced the explosion down.

Chase watched Frazier for a beat. "You okay?"

"I want you to clear his name."

"I'm already looking into it."

"Looking into it is not good enough. I want it done, the sooner the better, before the NBA teams take him off their draft boards."

"Okay. I get it."

Frazier looked out the window past Chase. Chase followed his gaze. Kendrick stood on the sidewalk, looking totally out of place. Even in a city as dark and menacing as Detroit, Kendrick looked out of place. Chase wondered just where he *would* fit in.

"Kendrick is a good kid," Frazier said. "Like a lot of football players, he has problems controlling his aggression off the field. Now, well, he doesn't have the field to get out that aggression. So I tend to have a hard time controlling him." He shook his head. "The kid had the physical ability, but he struggled to understand the playbook. You can't play in the NFL if you don't know what you're doing, so he washed out. But he is still meaner than hell and strong. I'd take him in a fight with a grizzly bear."

"Okay," Chase said again, "message received."

Frazier backed off the rhetoric a little and said, "I'll make it worth your while."

Chase nodded. "I need to talk to Bowe. Do you know where he is?"

"Of course."

Andy Clinton sat in the visitor chair while Dick Northern sat behind the desk. Northern's chair was turned and he stared out the window. Clinton looked at him in profile. They were about the same age, but Northern had an aura about him that made Clinton cede power. Northern also outranked him, but it was the dangerous vibes that radiated from him that did the trick. Like a supervillain from the comics, Northern would stop at nothing to accomplish whatever goal he had set. The fact that he wore a police uniform just made him all the scarier. He had steely blue eyes and a shaved head. His face was hard angles lined deep around his mouth and between his eyes.

"What happened to your face?" Northern said, still looking out the window.

Clinton fidgeted in the chair. The last thing he wanted

was to look weak to Northern. "Chase," he said. "He sucker-punched me."

"Really?"

Clinton fidgeted some more. "Yes, really."

"So you can corroborate that the girl was with the basketball player?"

"Yes," Clinton said, caught off-guard by the sudden change of direction. "Another person who was at the party, one of his teammates actually." He thought about the interview with Deon Henderson. What the hell did that kid have in that bedroom?

It was like Northern could read his mind. "A teammate? Why would he throw Bradlee under the bus? Did you threaten him?"

Clinton was glad Northern wasn't facing him. "Didn't have to." He knew he was a terrible liar.

Northern spun the chair and faced him. "I don't care how you got the information, Andy. You just need to be sure it'll stand up in court. If the kid recants or claims he was coerced, you'll be shit out of luck."

Clinton set his jaw. "It'll stand up."

Northern nodded. "So, you have them together. How do you know they stayed together? And how'd he get her to that empty lot?"

"He could have taken her there after everybody left," Clinton said. "Hell, he could have waited until the next day. She wasn't very big. He could have stuck her in a laundry sack and carried her out of the room like he was going to do laundry."

"Is that what happened?"

Clinton shrugged. "I don't know."

Northern's eyes bored a hole through Clinton. "You have to find out, Andy. Just putting them together isn't enough. She was probably seen with several people. It was a party, remember?"

"Okay, Dick," Clinton said. "I'll get it."

Northern nodded and turned back to the window.

Clinton was being dismissed, but he had another problem. "Uh, Dick?"

"Yes, Andy," Northern said, forcing himself to remain calm.

"I've been thinking. Strangulation is a pretty up-close thing."

"It is."

"So, what I'm wondering is if he were that close to her, did she scratch him or anything like that? Maybe we can get DNA from under her fingernails."

Northern turned back to Clinton. "Excellent thought, Andy." He picked up the desk phone and punched in a number. "Stan," he said into the phone, "Dick Northern. Listen, the ah… what's her name, Sergeant?"

"Beach."

"The Beach girl," Northern continued into the phone. "Did you get scrapings from under the nails?" He paused while the County Medical Examiner, Stan Burwell, responded. "Good. Have you run DNA?" Northern paused again. "Okay, listen, Stan, nobody but Sergeant Clinton or I get those results. Understand? Nobody. These are 'eyes only'—you, me and Sergeant Clinton. The results are not to be left unattended anywhere—not on a desk, in an unlocked file cabinet, on an unsecured computer, anywhere. Got it?" He nodded while he listened to the reply. "Good. I know I can count on you, Stan." He hung up and looked at Clinton. "Anything else?"

Clinton shook his head.

Northern turned back to the window to think about whatever dastardly deed he was working on next. "Oh, and Andy," he said, "drop the charges against Chase."

Clinton was dumbfounded. "But—"

"It makes you look like a pussy, Andy. You got a

problem with the man, settle it, but don't make the department look bad because you got your ass kicked."

Chapter 18

Rumor had it that Pudge Rodriguez had signed with the Tigers in 2004 at the behest of his wife. She remembered the shopping in the Birmingham area from previous trips to Detroit. When the Tigers made a free-agent offer to Pudge, she jumped at the chance to actually live there. They divorced two years later so maybe moving to Detroit hadn't been such a great idea, or maybe it had nothing at all to do with it.

Birmingham was about twenty miles north of Detroit, straight up the Chrysler Freeway. It, along with neighbors Bloomfield Hills, Beverly Hills and Royal Oak, made up one of the most affluent areas in the country. Not coincidentally, Birmingham was also one of the Midwest's premier shopping districts, featuring somewhere around 300 retail stores in an area of less than five square miles.

Chase entered the Townsend Hotel in Birmingham just after noon and rode the elevator to the top floor. Bowe's suite was at the end of the corridor. He found the door and knocked. When no reply came, he pounded harder.

"Who the fuck is it?" a muffled, Barry-White-like voice asked from inside the suite.

"My name is Chase."

"Don't know no fuckin' Chase."

"There's no reason you should, but I'm here to help you."

The door was yanked open, and Chase found himself looking at a chest that filled the opening. It appeared to be carved from a piece of onyx. He had to tip his head back to see the face that hovered at least nine inches above his head. Every inch of the man was long and muscled. He looked like a sculpture over at the Detroit Institute of Art. His head was

107

shaved, and the dim light from the hallway shone off it like the golden tower of the Fisher Building. A beard that barely showed against the black skin edged a scowling face. He wore warm-up pants and no shirt.

His eyes scanned Chase from top to bottom, scrutinizing every inch. If looks could kill, Chase would have dropped dead right there in the hallway.

"What I need help with?" he said when his inspection was complete.

Chase looked up and down the hall. They were alone, but he still felt exposed. "Can we go in the room?"

"Some white guy looks like a cop shows up at my door, and I'm just supposed to let him into my room? What's this about anyway?"

"Aley Beach."

The name brought no recognition to his face. "Who?"

"The girl you allegedly killed."

A light finally shone in Bowe's eyes. "Oh, shit, you the dude Howard said was comin' to see me."

Chase breathed a sigh of relief. "Right."

"Why din't you say so?"

"I don't know," Chase said. "I guess I'm not that bright."

"Well, what you doin' here? Why ain't you out investigatin'? Findin' out who did it?"

"I need to start with your side of the story."

"Ain't got no side. Din't even know the bitch."

"Why don't you let me in, and we can talk about it."

Bowe looked over his shoulder and then shrugged and stepped aside. It was as if another door had opened. A small living room with a couch and two facing chairs fronted a fireplace. A red tee-shirt, roughly the size of a circus tent, was draped over one of the chairs. A black halter-type dress and a lacy white thong lay on the couch. A mirror lay on the coffee table with traces of white powder and a rolled-up hundred- dollar bill on it. An empty champagne bottle under the coffee table completed the scene.

"Are we having a party?" Chase asked.

"Just some ho up in here last night," Bowe said. "You know how it is."

Chase didn't know how it was but didn't let on. He didn't want Bowe to think he wasn't cool. One side of a set of glass-paneled French doors set into the opposite wall opened and a redhead walked out, naked as the day she was born. Her skin was pale white, and it was obvious from her lady area that she was a real redhead. She yawned and stretched with the grace of a cat. "Have you seen my cigarettes, Bowe?" she asked. If she noticed Chase, she didn't let on.

"You got to go," Bowe said.

"In a minute. I have to shower and dress, but right now I need a cigarette."

"You got to go, now," Bradlee insisted, wrapping one of his huge hands around her upper arm. He pulled her across the suite toward the door.

The redhead stumbled, trying to keep pace with his much-longer strides. "Wait a minute. What about my clothes?"

"Yo," Bowe called to Chase. "Little help?"

Chase scooped up the dress and thong and brought them to the door. Bowe opened the door, shoved the redhead into the hall, took the clothes from Chase, flung them into the hall after her and slammed the door.

The woman banged on the door. "What about my cigarettes?"

Bowe walked to the coffee table and snatched the rolled-up hundred off the mirror. He returned to the door and threw it into the hall. "Buy some more," he said and then turned to Chase. "Now, what the fuck you want?"

His glare was meant to intimidate. People his size were used to being intimidating. Chase wasn't intimidated and felt it important to show that, to put them on even ground. So he walked to the couch and sat down. The redhead's perfume had settled on the couch and was now settling on him. It's tough to be tough when you smell like a stripper, but he gave it his best shot. He crossed his legs and said, "Aley Beach."

Bowe didn't move from his spot next to the door. He folded his massive arms across the expanse of chest, looking like an African god. "What about her?"

Chase sighed. This was going nowhere fast. "The night you guys won your conference tournament and got into the NCAA tournament."

"What about it?" Bowe smiled at the memory. "I dropped twenty-three and fifteen that night. Beat the shit outta them white boys from Wisconsin."

Chase nodded. "Good, glad you remember. Now how about the party afterward? You remember that?"

"Oh yeah," Bowe said. The smile widened, displaying impossibly white teeth. "We *partied* that night."

"Do you remember the girl you were with that night?"

"You think I remember all the hos I been with? Shit, they all want a piece of this." He cupped his crotch like a super-sized Michael Jackson.

"Nice," Chase said, shaking his head. "So you have no idea what happened to Aley that night?"

"Naw, man. All I remember is we had a good time, partied all night."

"Did you have sex that night?"

Bowe grinned like the cat that ate the canary. "I usually do."

"Do you remember who with?"

"Not really." Bowe thought for a few moments. "Oh, wait. White girl, I think."

"Could it have been Aley Beach?"

Bowe shrugged. "I don't know who that is."

Chase sighed again and pulled the picture of Aley from his pocket. He held it up for Bowe to see and said, "This girl?"

Bowe studied the picture and said, "Could have been. I probably would have done her if the opportunity had presented itself."

"So you don't remember if you had sex with her, but you're sure you didn't kill her and dump her body in an empty lot?"

"Look, man—" Bowe dropped the act "—I have sex with lots of girls. I don't remember them all. Okay? Maybe that makes me a dick or whatever, but I did not kill anybody. I would have remembered that."

Chase nodded. "Okay. But if you didn't do anything, why are you hiding?"

"Some racist cop trying to hang this thing on me."

"How's that?"

"How's what?"

"How's he trying to hang it on you?"

"He just is," Bowe said. "You watch. Fuckin' cracker gonna put it on me for sure."

"Have you been having any trouble with anyone? Is there any reason someone would want to accuse you of this?"

Bowe shook his head. "I don't know anything. All I do is play ball and party from time to time. There's no reason someone would want to put this on me, other than me being black."

"What about your brother?"

Bowe scowled. "What about him?"

"Could he have done this? Maybe he thought he was protecting you from something?"

"From what?"

"I don't know. Is there anything he might have needed to protect you from?"

"Naw, man," Bowe said. "I don't need no protection. Nothing that would lead to a girl's death."

Chase nodded his head and got up to leave. It was clear

to him that Bowe had no idea what had happened to Aley.

Laura Phillips' cell phone rang as she was just about to walk out the door. She was on top of the world following the national broadcast she had participated in. Her cell phone had not stopped ringing with congratulatory calls and texts from family, friends and former teammates. She was on her way to her day job with the Tigers, which was a bit of a letdown at that point; but for the first time since she had taken the job, she could see herself working her way out of it. Brad Hamilton had been pleased with her performance. The network had been flooded with calls from viewers wanting to know who the new girl was, and her agent was already getting calls from other networks throwing out feelers. So it was quite a surprise when the caller screamed, "What the hell was that?" in her ear.

It was the pig. He continued before Laura could respond. "I told you NOT to pursue that story. And you went around my back and did it anyway? Who the hell do you think you are?"

For the first time since she had met the man, Laura was not intimidated. "You're right," she said. "I did go behind your back. It's a good story and you were incapable of seeing that, so I found someone who was."

The pig sputtered into the phone, trying to make words. "Well guess what, missy," he finally managed to say, "as of right now, you are suspended. And you can be damn sure that I will do everything within my power to make sure that you get fired."

"Okay. I don't think you actually have the power to suspend me. I'll have to check with my agent, if she can carve out a couple of minutes between all the calls she's receiving with offers for my services. In the meantime, you can go fuck yourself."

More sputtering came from the pig, and Laura hung up

on him. She threw her hands in the air and stomped her feet in a celebratory dance. She couldn't remember the last time she had been that happy. She immediately changed course and went to look for Bowe Bradlee.

She entered O'Ryan's ten minutes later. It was dimmer than she had remembered. She stood just inside the entrance, waiting for her eyes to adjust. She wore blue jeans, an oversized U of M sweatshirt, a navy-blue ball cap with a yellow block M and a pair of Nike running shoes. She hadn't been this comfortable in a long time.

A man at a table to her left called out to her, "Hey, you look like that girl on TV that does the Tigers games."

"Really?"

"Yeah, except she's better-looking."

Laura smiled and nodded. "Thanks."

The man didn't respond. He had already gone back to concentrating on his beer. Laura looked around the room. She didn't see Chase. She walked to the bar and climbed onto a stool. On the TV above the bar, Chris McKendry from ESPN was talking about Bowe Bradlee. Laura screamed on the inside. She had scooped ESPN!

The older gentleman behind the bar ambled over. He looked at her and smiled. "Anybody ever tell you you look like that girl on TV that does the Tigers games?"

Laura hooked her thumb over her shoulder like a hitchhiker in the general direction of the guy at the table. "That guy over there just did. Except he said she was better-looking than me.

The bartender looked over her shoulder and then waved his hand in a dismissive gesture. "Don't listen to him. He's drunk."

Laura smiled. "Can you keep a secret?"

"No."

Laura laughed. "I'm actually her. Laura Phillips."

The bartender tipped his head back and looked at her

with more deliberation, then shook his head. "Nah. You're close, I'll give you that. But you aren't her."

"Why can't I be her?"

"Because if you were, you sure as hell wouldn't be in this place."

"Okay," Laura said. "I'll concede that point. Is Chase around?"

The bartender shook his head. "No."

"Do you know when he'll be back?"

"No. But he'll turn up sooner or later."

"You sure?"

"Yep. He lives here. He'll come home sometime. Can I help you with something?"

"Do you know where Bowe Bradlee's brother lives?"

"No."

"Then I'm afraid not," Laura said. "I need to find him."

Chapter 19

Chase returned to O'Ryan's more confused than ever. He had absolutely no idea who had killed Aley Beach. He didn't even have a viable suspect.

Ty Jackson had asked him to find Bowe and make sure he was safe. Chase had found him and he seemed safe. He could report that to Ty and let the police handle the murder investigation. However, Bowe was right. Clinton *was* a racist, and he was out to hang the murder on Bowe. And it wouldn't be hard to do so because at that point, Bowe was the most likely suspect.

There was also that other thing involving Howard Frazier and Kendrick Martin. Frazier was determined that Bowe would be the first pick in the draft, come hell or high water. Chase had absolutely no proof that Frazier had been involved in any way with Aley's disappearance and murder, but he wouldn't be surprised if that's how it turned out. Absent any proof to the contrary, Bowe was in the crosshairs.

He was thinking these things while nursing a beer. Sarge turned on the Tigers' game. Chase looked up from his thoughts long enough to recognize that the guy doing the pre-game was not Laura Phillips—it really wasn't that difficult for a detective of Chase's ilk to figure out.

"I wonder why Laura's not doing the pre-game," Chase wondered aloud.

Sarge turned to him and said, "That the blonde girl who does the pre-game stuff?"

"That's right."

Sarge laughed. "Some girl claiming to be her stopped in earlier, looking for you."

"Did she say *why* she was looking for me?" Chase said.

"She said something about going to look for Bowe's

brother," Sarge said in a dismissive tone.

Chase choked on his beer. "Shit! Where's Sally? Sally!"

Sally came out of the backroom, looking irritated. "What are you yelling about?"

"What'd you find out about Bowe's family? Tell me he has more than the one brother."

"I've been looking," Sally said. "There's a lot of stuff to sift through online, mostly game reviews and stats and stuff."

"Sally," Chase said, "does he have more than one brother?"

"I found an article that mentioned that he spent his last two years of high school living with his coach, after the grandmother who he had been living with died. His father is out of his life, and his mother is a crack addict, probably living on the streets."

"Brothers?"

Sally nodded. "He has a brother who's a gang member."

Chase nodded. "Atari Black. Are there any others?"

"That's all I've found so far."

"Shit."

Laura Phillips had gone looking for a gang member in Detroit. Chase really hoped she didn't find him.

Contrary to popular belief, Detroit is not all ghetto. There are a few decent places to live in the city. The Lafayette Park area is one such place. It was where Ty Jackson lived with his wife Wanda. Chase literally ran from O'Ryan's and jumped in the Charger. It was only a few blocks but seemed to take forever. He had an uneasy feeling in the pit of his stomach.

The Pavilion Apartment building was a high-rise that overlooked the park. Chase parked in the driveway in front of the glass front doors and rode the elevator up to the tenth floor. He pounded on the door of the Jacksons' apartment and pounded and pounded until Ty finally opened.

"Chase," Ty said, relieved. "My God, we thought

someone was trying to break down the door."

"Ty, listen," Chase said, not listening to Ty. "I need to know where to find Bowe's brother."

"You think Bowe is with his brother?" He sounded concerned about that.

"No. I know where Bowe is. He's fine."

"Then what's this about?"

"There's a lady, a reporter. I think she's in trouble. I think she went to try and find Bowe's brother to try and find Bowe."

"That's not good," Jackson said. "He's with the BD Boyz."

"I know. That's why I'm freaking out."

"Come in and let's figure this out," Ty said. He sounded a lot like a teacher, which, of course, he was. He led Chase into a small living room with a remarkable view of downtown Detroit and the Renaissance Center. Nobody standing in that room and looking at that view would believe they were in Detroit.

Wanda Jackson appeared from wherever she had been hiding. She was a striking woman. She wasn't what one would call a natural beauty, but there was something about her. She had latte skin and an athlete's body. Her shoulders were just a bit too wide and her butt and legs just a bit too thick, but she exuded sexy. She was dressed conservatively, as she was a teacher, as well; but she turned it into a "hot for teacher" way. The look she gave Chase didn't convey sexy. It conveyed her desire to kick his ass.

"Chase!" she said when she saw who had been banging on the door. "You scared us half to death."

"I'm sorry for the intrusion," Chase said, "but this is urgent. This lady is in danger. I need to know what you know about Bowe's brother."

"The white lady that reported about the dead girl and implied that Bowe had something to do with it?" Wanda said with disdain.

"She didn't imply that Bowe had anything to do with it. She simply said he was someone the police had talked to and wanted to talk to again. And yes, her."

"Do you know where Bowe is?"

"Yes, he's safe."

"Did you tell *her* where he is?"

"No, I didn't, which is why she went looking for his brother to try to find Bowe, I guess. I actually don't know why she wanted to find him, but I assume it was to see if he knew where Bowe was."

"Bowe's not with Atari, is he?" Ty asked, again with genuine concern.

"No," Chase said. "He's in a hotel in Birmingham."

"Birmingham?" Wanda said. "What's he doing in Birmingham?"

Chase shrugged. "That's where his agent got him a room."

"Agent?" the Jacksons said in unison.

"Howard Frazier."

"Howard Frazier," Ty moaned.

"Who's Howard Frazier?" Wanda wanted to know.

"He's an agent," Ty said. "A sleaze who hangs around the high schools and colleges. I don't have proof, but I'm pretty sure he pays players to get them indebted to him, so he can sign them when they turn pro. Is that what he did with Bowe?"

"Yes," Chase said. "He told me he has 'owned' Bowe since the eighth grade."

Ty shook his head. "Dumb kid. I told him, hell, I told all of my kids to stay away from Frazier."

"He had his hooks into him long before you came along, Ty," Chase said. "Anyway, Bowe's fine right now. I need to find the reporter."

Ty sighed. "The BD Boyz still hang around the project. I have no idea where Atari sleeps, but I'm pretty sure you can find him over there."

Chase thanked Ty for the information and headed for the door.

"Wait," Ty said. "You can't go there alone."

Chapter 20

The Brewster-Douglass housing project had been the first federally-financed housing project in the country. First Lady Eleanor Roosevelt had broken ground for the construction in 1935. At peak capacity, it had housed 8,000-10,000 people in six fifteen-story high-rises and two six-story low-rises spread over a fifteen-square-block area on the east side in the Brush Park section of the city. Many notable Detroiters, including Diana Ross, Smokey Robinson and Mary Wilson had lived there. By 2008, only 280 families still lived in the apartments. Both of the low-rises had been torn down as had two of the high-rises. The city had made the decision to shut the project down for good but hadn't gotten around to razing the four remaining towers. They had stood empty ever since. Just another blight on the city.

Chase wasn't dumb enough to go to Brewster-Douglass alone, but he hadn't planned on taking Ty Jackson with him. His plans didn't seem to matter though because Ty had followed him down to the car and jumped into the passenger seat. Chase didn't have the time to argue with him, so he dropped the car into drive and pushed the accelerator to the floor.

"What's the plan?" Ty said, bracing himself with hand on the ceiling as they blasted through the intersection of Russell and Gratiot, catching air, Dukes-of-Hazzard style.

Chase tried to keep his focus on the road. The last thing he needed at that point was to be involved in a traffic accident. "Don't have one. I guess we'll just wing it."

Ty mumbled "great" under his breath. Chase took it as a sign that Ty was regretting his snap decision to come along. He didn't hold it against him. If he had taken the time to think it through, he would have probably regretted his decision to go as well.

Chase had learned it was better not to think of the danger but to prepare for it at the same time. In that vein, he had called Mo Warrick and requested backup as they tore up Chrysler Drive, passing cars on a double yellow line. He skidded through a left at Mack and eased to a stop in the shadow of the derelict housing project. Two cops climbed out of a blue and white squad car as they arrived

The passenger was an older guy. He wore a black cop sweater with patches on the shoulders and elbows over body armor. He was black with a thin mustache and the seen-it-all cop's eyes. The driver was a younger guy with biceps on full display under a short-sleeved uniform shirt. He was tough but not dumb; he wore body armor as well.

"You Chase?" the older cop said as Chase climbed from the Charger.

"Yep," Chase said, walking to the trunk. He popped the lid and extracted an Ithaca pump shotgun. He already had a Beretta M9 on his hip.

"Whoa!" the young guy said, reaching for his sidearm.

"Easy," Chase said, racking the slide and chambering a round. "I'm not the bad guy."

The older guy hadn't flinched, but he hadn't taken his eyes off the shotgun either. "Want to tell us what's going on? We got a call saying a civilian was in need of assistance."

Chase filled his jacket pockets with extra shells and an extra clip for the Beretta. "I need you to cover my ass," he said. And don't let him get shot." He nodded his head at Ty Jackson. "His wife will kill me if anything happens to him."

"Going to war?" the older cop said.

Chase smiled, showing more bravado than he felt. "I was a Boy Scout. Always prepared."

"A Boy Scout?"

"Okay, I was only a Cub Scout. I didn't like camping in the snow. But I subscribe to the 'Always Prepared' model."

121

Chase turned to the housing project. If a filmmaker wanted to shoot a post-Apocalyptic movie, this would be the place to do it. The towers loomed empty, dark and menacing. There was not a piece of glass left in any of the windows. Graffiti covered the brick walls like billboards. Piles of rubble dotted the landscape. Weeds pushed through the cracked pavement that covered the grounds. Netless basketball hoops stood unused and alone.

Nothing moved. Literally. The wind was still. The weeds stood straight. Chase didn't even see a fly or a moth. And yet he had the feeling that someone was watching them. He couldn't tell from where. There were literally hundreds of windows facing them. A sniper could have been set up in any one of them.

"You want to tell us what's going on here?" the old cop said.

"I'm looking for a woman. I was told she came here looking for Atari Black."

"Shit," the young guy said. "You're going to mess with the BD Boyz?"

"If need be."

"Wait," Ty said, placing his hand on the barrel of the shotgun.

He stepped off the curb, crossed the street and limped to the center of the basketball court. He placed his hands next to his mouth in a makeshift megaphone and yelled Atari's name.

The two officers took up positions on the far side of their patrol car. The young guy had his pistol drawn. The older cop had the shotgun from the patrol car. Both were using the car's roof to steady their aim on the towers.

Chase stood in the middle of the street. His hand held the shotgun by the pistol grip, his finger wrapped around the trigger.

"Atari!" Ty yelled a second time. "Come on out. We

don't need any blood shed here today."

They all waited for what seemed like hours. Finally, a lone figure appeared from the nearest tower. It was hard to tell much other than color from across the vast emptiness. He was black and lanky. The proportion to the door that he exited from made him look tall. It could have been a short door, but probably not. He moved with an easy grace toward Ty. Chase stepped up on the curb and walked slowly toward Ty as well.

It was then that another man appeared from the tower, followed closely by another. The first man, presumably Atari, was empty-handed. The followers weren't.

"Shit!" Chase heard the young cop say again.

They all converged on Ty within seconds of each other. The two gun hands both carried machine pistols, Tec-9s or something similar. Chase didn't take the time to inspect them, but he was pretty sure the guns were illegal. His police backup didn't seem too interested in disarming them.

"What the fuck you doin', Coach?" Atari said.

"We're looking for a young lady," Ty said.

"A white girl?"

"Yes."

Atari shook his head. "Ain't seen no white girl round here."

"Bullshit," Chase said.

Atari turned his eyes to him. Until then, he hadn't given any indication that he knew Chase was even there. "You calling me a liar, Casper?"

"If the shoe fits."

"I tol' you, I ain't seen no white bitch."

"Then how did you know we were looking for one?"

"Why else a mothafuckin' white boy come out here? And with 5-0 back up. You sure ain't lookin' for no sister."

"Fuck you!" Chase said.

Atari's gun hands startled.

"Okay," Ty said in his coach voice. "Everybody take it down a notch."

Atari's eyes never left Chase, but he spoke to Ty, "All due respect, Coach, but you on *my* court. I the one decides who 'take it down a notch.'"

"Understood," Ty said. "But we're trying to help your brother. The lady we're looking for was supposed to have been looking for you in an effort to find Bowe. We just want to make sure she's safe."

"I tol' you—"

"I know," Ty said, trying like hell to contain the situation.

Chase was a little worked up and didn't help. "What do you know about the murder of the girl Bowe was seen with?" he said.

"Oh, so now I killed that bitch too?" Atari said.

"She worked for you. She could have come up short. Or maybe Bowe raped her like the police are saying, and you killed her so she wouldn't ruin his draft stock. But you fucked up. His being mentioned at all is already ruining his draft stock. You should have paid her off instead of killing her."

Atari lunged at Chase. "Motherfucker!"

Chase shoved the barrel of the shotgun into Atari's chest to stop him. One of the gun hands squeezed his trigger and sent a three-shot burst into the air. Chase had no idea how nobody got hit. The young cop returned fire, but he didn't hit anything either.

Atari froze for a second, probably shocked that Chase had jabbed the shotgun into his chest. Chase took the opportunity to bust him in the jaw with the butt of the shotgun. Atari went down in a heap, and Chase trained the gun on the gun hands.

"Don't fucking move. I promise I won't miss."

They both looked from him to Atari and back.

"Put the guns down," Chase said.

They hesitated. He screamed, "Now!" and fired a round over their heads.

There's not a shadow of a doubt that those young men were hardened criminals and were not the least bit afraid of Chase, but there's something about the roar of a shotgun that will stop even the biggest bad-ass in his tracks. The machine pistols rattled to the pavement before the roar ended.

"Pick 'em up, Ty," Chase said.

Ty didn't move. Chase snuck a peek out of the corner of his eye. Ty was rattled. He had grown up on the streets of Detroit but apparently had been in that comfy park-side apartment a little too long.

"Ty… " Chase said, a little more urgently than he had intended.

Ty slowly leaned down and picked up the machine pistols.

"Now go," Chase told him.

Ty limped toward the car as fast as his messed-up leg would take him. Chase walked backward as fast as he could while keeping the shotgun trained on the two gun hands and hoping that a sniper shot didn't come from one of the empty windows in the towers. Atari pushed up to his hands and knees. A line of blood ran from his mouth and pooled on the basketball court. Chase was going to have to watch his back for a while.

Chapter 21

The cops held cover for Chase and Ty until they reached the Charger. All four men loaded into the two cars and got the hell out of there before the BD Boyz organized a counter assault. They met up again a few blocks away.

The older cop exploded as he climbed from the patrol car. "What the hell was that?"

Ty stayed in the Charger. Chase exited the driver's seat and turned to the cops, showing more pluck than he actually felt. "Thanks for the backup. That almost got out of hand."

"Almost?"

Chase handed him the machine pistols. "Relax. Everybody is okay. Why don't you take these back to your station, check them for prints and run them through ballistics? I have a suspicion that they'll match an unsolved crime or two."

The cop shook his head in disbelief at Chase's demeanor. "You know I'll have to report where I got them from."

"Feel free to take the credit," Chase said.

"And what do I say when I'm asked why I didn't arrest the young men who owned them?"

Chase shrugged. "You'll think of something."

"Yeah, the truth." He turned back to the patrol car, popped the trunk and secured the machine pistols. He closed the trunk with a thump and smiled. "The truth shall set you free."

Chase dropped Ty back at his apartment. By the time he reached O'Ryan's, his adrenaline had subsided enough for his nerves to catch up; and a huge aftershock of anxiety from the experience had kicked in. His heartbeat raced at about 300 beats per minute, and he trembled from head to toe.

He was shocked when he found Laura Phillips sitting at the bar, chatting with Sally. Both women looked up when he said, probably a little too loudly, "What are you doing here?"

"I work here," Sally said.

"Not you." He pointed a shaky finger at Laura Phillips. "Her."

"I need to talk to you," Laura said.

"Son of a bitch! I just almost got killed looking for you, and you're sitting here?"

"What are you talking about? Where have you been?" Sally asked.

"Over at Brewster-Douglass, looking for her."

"Why would you look for her there?"

Chase looked at Sarge. He had his head down, working a crossword puzzle, ignoring them. "Because Sarge told me she was going looking for Bowe's brother."

"I was," Laura said, "but I didn't know where to look. That's what I wanted to talk to you about. What's Brewster-Douglass?"

Chase ignored the question. "I did you a favor this morning, and you go on TV and say Bowe killed her?"

"What did you think I was going to do? Besides, I didn't say Bowe killed her."

"You might as well have."

"That was a national broadcast," she said. There was a sparkle in her eyes. "That was my chance at going to the big time."

"By ruining this kid's life?"

"Chase," Sally said, "take a breath."

He did. Adrenaline pumped through his veins at roughly the speed of light. His body struggled to keep up with the emotions that bounced him from pillar to post.

"What happened at Brewster-Douglass?" Sally continued. "Are you okay?"

"I went there looking for her and had a little confrontation with the BD Boyz. I ended up hitting the leader in the mouth with the butt of a shotgun."

"Are you crazy?" Sally said.

"I thought she was in danger," Chase shot back. Another aftershock of the shakes hit him, racking his entire body. "Son of a bitch!"

"Drink this," Sarge said, sliding a shot glass in front of him.

Chase drank it in one gulp and slammed the glass down on the bar. Jack Daniels. It burned all the way down, but his heart began to slow and a trace of calm came over him.

"Thanks."

"Don't mention it," Sarge said and went back to his puzzle.

"Bowe didn't do it," Chase said. He didn't really *know* that, but he would be damned if he were going to let this lady help Clinton railroad the kid. "And if you help Clinton railroad this kid, it's going to destroy your career, not help it."

"How do you know Bowe didn't do it?" Laura Phillips said.

"I talked to him."

"You did? You know where he is?"

Chase shook his head with a chuckle. "Lady, I'm not telling you shit."

"But if I could talk to him, I—"

"No!"

"Come on," Laura said. "I broke this thing. They're all chasing me now: ESPN, Fox, NBC, Mike and Mike, Jim Rome, all of them. They're all talking about *my* story."

Chase shook his head again. "I'll admit, I was taken in by your beauty. You got me, okay? You batted your eyelashes at me and I helped you. But that almost got me killed, and now I've probably got a fucking bounty on my head. Uh-uh. No more. You're on your own."

Laura listened with her mouth hanging open. She had probably never been rebuffed by a man in her life. It took a second for it to sink in, and then she said, "Fine!" She slid off the stool, then stomped across the floor and out the door.

Chase watched her leave. The adrenaline left with her, and he deflated like a balloon. He climbed onto the stool that the reporter had vacated, feeling like an anchor was tied to his back.

Sally watched him closely. "Are you okay?" she said.

"I'll live."

"As long as the BD Boyz don't catch up to you."

Chase laughed in spite of himself. "True dat."

"So what's your next move?"

"I'm not sure. I'd like to know how Aley Beach's body got from the party to that empty lot."

"Is that important?"

"It is if somebody saw Bowe Bradlee, or preferably somebody else, carry a dead body out of the dorm."

Chapter 22

Chase had a thought. He took his cell phone out of his pocket and punched in the number for the DPD. After getting bounced around a couple of times, he finally managed to get Andy Clinton on the phone.

"Andy, my man," he said, "I got a question for you."

"Fuck you, Chase!" Andy said.

Chase ignored the insult. "Anyway, I'm wondering how Aley Beach got from Bowe Bradlee's dorm to the empty lot where she was found."

Andy didn't make a sound.

"You still there?" Chase asked.

"Fuck you!"

"Okay, good. I thought you had hung up. So, do you have any info on how the body was moved?"

"Fuck you, Chase!" Clinton said. This time he did hang up.

"I guess he doesn't have any info on how the body was moved," Chase said to Sally as he put the phone back in his pocket.

Chase was laughing, but Sally wasn't. "I guess this little incident didn't do anything to alleviate your fears about my safety," he said.

She barked out an ironic laugh. "Nope, can't say it did."

Chase felt like an ass for making her worry. "Let me tell you a story," he said. "I was in love once—"

"*You*?"

"I know, hard to believe."

"I'll say."

"Anyway, her name was Paige. We were just kids. I was hardly out of the academy on my first assignment after leaving my training with Sarge. My partner was a hard-on named Dick Northern."

"Good name for a hard-on," Sally said.

Chase nodded. "True. Anyway, Paige worked as a teller in a bank. Dick and I stopped there one afternoon to cash our pay checks. I was excited because I was going to go after work to make the final lay-away payment on the engagement ring I was going to give her."

"Engagement ring?"

"Yeah. So, I waited in Paige's line for her. When I got up there, we chatted a little, maybe flirted a little as well. Then Dick and I left.

"I had no more than opened the door to our patrol car when we heard a shotgun blast from inside the bank. It was being robbed. The sons of bitches had been in there with us and had waited for us to leave."

"Oh shit," Sally said, picking up on the tone of the story.

"I grabbed the radio and called it in," Chase said. "I wanted to wait for backup, but Dick was a cowboy. He fired on the bank and said we should charge the place, like he was having a flashback to Vietnam or something."

"You're kidding."

"I wish. The bank robbers had, of course, returned Dick's fire and blown out the bank's front window. Here I am, barely out of the academy. I hadn't even pulled my gun out of its holster at this point in my career, and there I was in the middle of a gunfight with bank robbers." He shook his head at the memory.

"Dick said, 'Let's go,' and charged the bank. What could I do? He was my partner, so I followed him."

"Oh my God," Sally said.

"We went in through the blown-out front window," Chase continued. "It was the only smart thing we did that day. If we had gone through the front door, they'd have picked us off like ducks in a shooting gallery.

"It was chaos inside the bank. Customers were lying on the ground, except for the few who had been too scared to move. Some had been shot in the gun battle, and the floor was slick with blood. Gun smoke hung in the air like fog.

"Dick took out one of the bad guys, and I got one. That left just one. He stood behind the teller counter with a shotgun pointed at Paige's head. Obviously, he had seen us flirting and figured she was his ticket out of there.

"'Drop your guns!' he shouted at us.

"'No way!' Dick replied. 'You drop yours!'

"'Let's all just calm down,' I said. I figured the backup would be arriving; and if we let this guy go, he'd walk right into their arms. 'Let him go, Dick,' I said.

"'I'm not dropping my gun,' Dick said. 'This fucker will shoot us all if we drop our guns.'

"I later learned the bank robber's name was Donald Woods. We negotiated a bit, believe it or not, and agreed that Dick and I would holster our weapons. I didn't know Dick well enough yet to know he couldn't be trusted to keep his word. Anyway, Woods and Paige made their way through the bodies still lying all over the floor toward the door. The shotgun was still pointed at Paige's head. Woods had a bag of money in his other hand.

"Dick let them pass and then pulled his gun and shot Woods in the head. Unfortunately, Woods's finger had been on the trigger, and he involuntarily jerked it when Dick's bullet entered his brain. The shotgun blast blew the back of Paige's head off."

"Oh my God, Chase!" Sally said. "That's horrible. I'm so sorry. How did you ever keep your jobs?"

Chase laughed. "Keep our jobs? The department and the city had to cover their asses; and since this was before the time of CNN and all the other vultures that happen to be feasting on Bowe's carcass at the moment, we not only kept our jobs but also received commendations and promotions. The department made us out to be heroes to thwart any civil suits from the families of the people who died."

132

"That's the most unbelievable thing I've ever heard."

"I was there and I still don't believe it," Chase said. "My point for telling you this story, however, is not to try and make you think I'm bullet-proof. My point is, even if you loved someone who worked in a bank instead of a patrol car, there's no guarantee he won't die on you. You can't live your life scared."

Sally placed her hand on Chase's chest and then let it fall away. "Thanks for sharing that with me, Chase," she said. "It's given me something to think about."

Chapter 23

Chase knocked on Bowe's dorm room door. Noise came from the other side of the door, but nobody answered. Why didn't these kids ever answer the damn door? He knocked harder.

"What?" somebody said from the other side.

It sounded like "come in," so Chase tried the knob. It was unlocked. Technically it was a dorm, but it was unlike any dorm he had ever been in. It was more of an apartment with a living room, a small kitchen, two bedrooms and a bathroom. It was decorated like a dorm, though. Posters of basketball players and women adorned the walls, along with memorabilia from D State Thunderbirds basketball.

A black kid, all arms and legs and elbows and knees, sat on a couch playing Madden. The tip of his tongue stuck out of the corner of his mouth. He wore the same black warmup pants that Bowe had worn, a gray sweatshirt and high-tops that were at least a size fifteen.

His name was Nic Langdon. He was a seven-foot center on the basketball team and Bowe's roommate. Chase looked at the gangly kid with his skinny legs stretched halfway across the living room. He'd have bet every one of the seven dollars in his pocket that, while a foot shorter than Langdon, Chase outweighed him.

"Who are you?" Langdon said. He concentrated on the game, his fingers a blur on the controller.

"My name is Chase. I'm investigating the murder."

"*What murder?*"

"The girl who disappeared from the party."

"She's dead?"

"Yes, she is," Chase said. Was it possible the kid didn't know? He sounded sincere.

Langdon shook his head and said, "Don't know nothin' 'bout that."

"Were you here that night?"

"I live here."

"So you were here?"

The kid looked at Chase out of the corner of his eye and then spoke in the same tone of all teenagers everywhere when talking to adults. "Yes, I was here."

Chase ignored the tone. "Did you happen to see the girl leave?"

"Nope."

"What about Bowe?"

"Nope."

"You didn't see Bowe leave the apartment that night?"

"Do I look like Bowe's mama? I don't watch his comings and goings."

Chase was fed up with the kid ignoring him. "No, you don't look like Bowe's mama. You look like his bitch, but not his mama."

That finally got Langdon's attention. He put down the controller and stood. He towered over Chase. "What'd you say to me?"

"Easy, slugger," Chase said. "I'm not here to fight with you. I'm just trying to figure out what happened to the girl."

"And I told you, I don't know." He said it slow and deliberate while leaning his face close to Chase's face.

Chase had an epiphany. He loved when that happened. Kids these days tape everything. "Do you know if anybody video-taped the party?"

"*Video taped?*"

Chase realized his error. "Well, you know, recorded it. Like on a cell phone." Not that he knew how to do that himself.

"I don't know," the kid said.

"Okay," Chase said, but he had talked his way into an idea.

In the hallway, he called Sally.

"Do you think you can pull up Facebook to see if anybody posted a video of the party?"

"Probably," Sally said. "Let me see what I can do."

Sally had a video all cued up for him by the time he got back to O'Ryan's.

"I found this on Facebook," she said. "It's posted on the page of a kid who was at the party. Apparently, he was proud of the keg stand he had done. I'm not so sure that his parents would be proud, but whatever."

She hit "play" on the video. A young man was aping for the camera, doing a really bad dance. His left arm crossed his chest, and he twirled an imaginary lasso over his head with his right.

"What the hell is he doing?"

"Gangnam Style," Sally said.

"What?"

"You know, Psy."

"Oh, sure," Chase said. He had no idea what she was talking about. *Psy?*

When the kid on the video was done with his lasso or whatever the hell he was using, he placed his hands on the handgrips of the keg and two other guys lifted his feet above his head while a third stuck the end of the hose in his mouth and squeezed the trigger. He drank for a few seconds and then his buddies let go of his legs, and he fell unceremoniously to the ground. After a few seconds, the kid popped up and threw his hands in the air and then started dancing again.

"Watch the upper right of the screen," Sally said, restarting the video.

Chase peeled his eyes off the idiot star of the video and focused where Sally indicated. A young lady staggered from the area where he knew the bedroom to be. She looked disoriented for a second and then made her way to the door. She was on the screen no more than a few seconds; and, because the video was focused on the idiot doing the keg stand, she was blurry. But Chase knew in his gut that it was Aley Beach.

"She left the apartment on her own," he said.

"So it would seem," Sally agreed. "But the video stops before we can see if anyone follows her."

"Maybe Mr. Keg Stand can tell us."

Chapter 24

Mr. Keg Stand's real name was John Busby. He lived in the same dorm as Aley Beach but on a different floor. Chase knocked on Busby's door bright and early the next morning. He waited somewhat impatiently until he heard movement inside the room.

"What?" Busby said, yanking open the door. He wore boxer shorts and no shirt. He was about Chase's height and built like he worked out with weights—not like Anthony Douglas, but few did.

"Are you supposed to be in class right now?" Chase said just for the hell of it.

The kid was irritated about being woken up. "I don't know." He rubbed his head, messing up the already messed-up bed-head. "What day is it?"

"Never mind. I need to talk to you about the party at Bowe Bradlee's dorm. Can I come in?"

"Can you... what?"

"Come in," Chase said, pushing Busby into the room. He followed and closed the door behind them.

"You can't—"

"I just did. Now tell me about the party. Did you have a good time?"

"I don't even know who you are," Busby whined. "You come pushing in here—"

"John," Chase said, "stop whining and concentrate. I saw the video of your keg stand on Facebook. I know you were at the party. I also know that Aley Beach was there. It was the last time she was seen alive. Do you want me to put the two of you together so it looks like you killed her?"

"Like I... what? I didn't kill anybody! I don't even know the girl!"

"I almost believe you, John. Now, what I need you to do is go down to the police station and show Sergeant Clinton the video you have posted on your Facebook page. Make sure he sees the girl in the upper right-hand corner of the shot. Got it?"

Confusion clouded the kid's face. "You want me to go to the police? And show them the video of me doing a keg stand?"

"Yes."

"I'm not going to do that."

Chase sighed. He had had just about all he could take from these damn college students. He pushed the kid against the wall and then pinned him to it with his forearm across the kid's cheek. His other cheek was against the wall, facing a calendar that featured pictures of the Detroit Pistons Cheerleaders.

"Yes, you are."

"Okay, shit, I'll do it," Busby said, his voice muffled from his face being pressed against the wall.

"Do what?" Chase said.

"I'll go down to the police station and show them the video."

"Show who?"

"Sergeant, um… Sergeant… "

"Clinton," Chase said, "like the president."

"Right, right. Clinton."

"Do it today, John. If you don't, I'm going to come back here and beat the shit out of you."

While he was there, Chase decided to stop by and see if Aley's roommate had remembered anything new, especially in light of the video. He knocked on the door to her room and got no answer. So he pounded harder and kept pounding until he heard a voice behind him, "You want to keep it down."

Chase turned to the voice and saw his old buddy, Todd

139

the RA, standing with his hands on his hips. He looked as if he had just gotten out of bed as well.

"Have you seen Rachel lately, Todd?"

Todd shook his head. "Not for a few days."

"Really?"

"Really."

Chase shook his head. "Does that alarm you? What with what happened to Aley Beach?"

"It's really not that unusual that I don't see them every day. I don't keep a watch out; I'm not a babysitter. Besides, they, like a lot of other college kids, often sleep in other places."

Damn this kid! He was right again. But the condescending tone of his voice irritated Chase. "Todd," he said, "if you say you're not a babysitter one more time, I'm going to knock your teeth out."

Todd stood there with a startled look on his face like he had been slapped.

"Do you have a key to her room?" Chase continued.

"No," Todd said like a chastised eight-year-old. "You'd have to get that from the Hall Director."

"Never mind." Chase stepped back from the door and kicked it. The boom raced down the corridor, bounced off the far wall and returned as the door frame exploded. The door swung in, bounced off the inside wall and swung back to a closed position.

Todd started to protest, but Chase was already into the room. It was empty except for two metal twin-sized bed frames with thin mattresses and a built-in double dresser/desk combination thing. There was nothing else in the room. Not even a stray piece of paper or a left-behind sock.

"When is the last time you saw her?"

Todd seemed more concerned about the broken door than the empty room. "I told you, a few days ago."

"Looks like she flew the coop."

"Ya think?"

"Where would she have gone?"

"I don't know. It's not like we were friends or anything."

Chase thought back to the conversation he had had with Rachel Corrigan. Where had she said she had come from? Port Huron! That was it.

"See ya, Todd," Chase said as he left the empty dorm room.

"Hey, you can't leave this door like this," Todd said to Chase's receding back.

Chapter 25

Port Huron is about an hour northeast of Detroit. Located at the southern end of Lake Huron, it is connected by the Blue Water Bridge to Point Edward, Ontario. It is the town where Thomas Edison grew up and worked as a news butcher as a young man, selling candy and newspapers on the train that ran between Port Huron and Detroit. A statue of a young Thomas Edison stands on the bank of the St. Clair River.

Chase jumped on I-94 and called Sally. He asked her to find the Corrigan house in Port Huron.

She called back with the address before he reached the city limits.

"By the way," she said after delivering the info, "Mo Warrick was in here looking for you."

"He was? Did he say what he wanted?"

"He said they got reports of a crazy man, fitting your description, destroying a dorm room over at D State."

Chase scoffed. *Fucking Todd.* "I'm sure that's an exaggeration."

"What'd you do, Chase?"

"Who said I did anything? Besides, it was only the door, not the whole room."

The large, white two-story house reminded Chase of the Cunninghams' house on "Happy Days." A long covered porch ran along the front of the house. A huge hedge stood sentry in front of that. The grass was still dormant from the cold spring, but the sunshine and warmer weather of the last few days had brought a few flowers out. He had no idea what kind of flowers they were, but he knew they were tough. They'd have to be to survive this early in the year.

He parked in the street in front of the house and took a

second to collect myself. He was worried. He didn't want to lose another teenage girl but didn't think he should kick in another door either, so he got himself under control before he approached the house.

As it turned out, Chase didn't need to kick in the door. Rachel Corrigan slowly swung on a swing suspended from the porch ceiling. She wore jeans and the same sweatshirt she had on the last time he had talked to her. One leg was folded under her, and the other hung down to the porch floor where she used her toe to push off. A cigarette burned between her fingers.

"I'm the truancy police," Chase said. "You're supposed to be in school."

Her smile was weak and ironic. Of course, it wasn't that great of a joke. "I'm taking a break," she said.

Chase pointed to a chair. "May I?"

She nodded and he sat.

"I was worried about you. I think Todd was too, but he's too cool to admit it."

Rachel shook her head at the mention of Todd. Chase was zero for two in the joke department.

"Aley left the party on her own," he said.

Rachel nodded. "She came home that night sometime between 2:30 and 3:00 a.m.."

"Why'd you tell everybody you last saw her with Bowe?"

Her hand shook as she brought the cigarette to her mouth and took a drag. "I was angry. Aley knew I had a thing for Bowe. I was nothing to him. I didn't get it at the time, but none of us were; he's so wrapped up in himself. But dammit, Aley knew how I felt about him, and she was my best friend."

Chase waited a beat for her to continue and then prompted, "What happened?"

"We had a huge fight and I threw her out."

"At 3 a.m.?"

Rachel grimaced. "I thought she'd go sleep it off in someone else's room, and we'd talk about it in the morning. But… she never came back."

"And you let everyone think she'd never made it home from the party?"

Rachel nodded. "I didn't know she was dead. I thought she'd show up sooner or later, and I was still so mad at her."

"And the suitcase?"

"That was dumb," she admitted. "I put some of her clothes in it and hid it in the trunk of my car. I don't know. I guess I thought it would look like she went away on her own."

"And then she turned up dead?"

"And I got scared."

"And ran home."

Rachel nodded and finished off the cigarette. She crushed the butt with her toe.

Chase shook his head and stood to leave.

"I never even said goodbye," Rachel said.

Chase turned back to her. "Wasn't it Peter Pan who said, 'Never say goodbye'?"

Rachel paused a beat and then finished the quote with a single tear rolling her cheek. "Because saying goodbye means going away, and going away means forgetting."

Clinton sat at his desk, thinking about his wife, Cheryl. The ache from missing her pained him to his core. She had been the one. Sure, he had screwed it up, but his actions didn't reflect his feelings. He would never love another person the way he loved Cheryl. He'd give anything for a chance to go back to the beginning and start over. He'd treat her like a queen. And he'd sure as hell not join the fucking Detroit Police Department. The thought of her with Chase was like a train wreck that he couldn't get out of his mind.

As much as he'd like to not think about it, it was present in his mind day and night.

The phone on his desk buzzed. "Shit," he said, reaching for it. He picked it up and barked, "Clinton!"

"This is Kelly at the front desk. You have a young man here to see you. He says he has information regarding the murder over at D State."

Clinton sat up straight. Could this be the break he'd been waiting for? Or something that was going to blow his case out of the water?

"Kelly," he said, "I'm on my way down. Do me a favor and stick him in a room."

He found John Busby in one of the phone-booth-sized rooms on the first floor off the main lobby. Physically he was a big kid and filled most of the small room. His knee bounced up and down like a jack hammer. He looked like he had seen a ghost. He had a bruise along his cheek bone, just below his right eye.

Clinton entered and sat across from the young man. "I'm Sergeant Clinton."

"Like the president," the kid said in a low voice.

"Right," Clinton said. "I hear you have some information for me?"

"Yeah, um, this guy came to my room and said I should bring you this." He placed a cell phone on the table between them.

Clinton looked at the phone, not wanting to touch it. "This guy, describe him."

The kid looked spooked. "Well, he was about your age. About six-foot, 200 pounds. In good shape for his age. Brown hair a little long. Goatee."

Chase, Clinton thought. "He do that to you?" Clinton said, pointing at the kid's cheek.

Busby touched the bruise tenderly. "Well, yeah."

"Do you want to press charges?"

"What? No," Busby said. "I just want to get this over with."

"Get what over with?"

"Well, like I said, this guy showed up at my dorm room and he knew about the video." Busby pointed at the phone on the table. "He wanted me to bring it down here and show you."

"Why did he hit you?"

Busby touched the bruise again. "He didn't really hit me. He just sort of shoved my face into the wall."

"Why?"

"I don't know. I guess I was being kind of a dick and told him I wouldn't bring the video down here."

"But you changed your mind?"

"Yeah, well, I don't want to get my ass kicked."

Definitely Chase, Clinton thought with a wry smile. "Well, let's see what you've got," he said.

Busby picked up the phone and pushed a couple of buttons and then turned the screen to Clinton. "The guy said to tell you to look in the upper right corner."

The screen was small, but Clinton saw it instantly even before Busby directed his attention to it. But was it really her? It was hard to tell, but he knew that Chase thought it was her. He had to defuse this right now.

"Do you know what you have there?" he asked the kid.

Busby shook his head. "I don't know anything. I swear."

"Watch it again," he told Busby. "Watch what the man told you to tell me to focus on."

Busby did as he was told and shrugged his shoulder. "I don't know what I'm looking at."

"The girl walking out the door. He thinks that's the girl who got killed."

"Whoa, wait a minute," Busby said. He watched the video again. "I don't know anything about that! I don't want to be involved in a murder!"

146

"Too late, kid," Clinton said. "You're involved. So tell me, after the girl left the party, did you see anybody follow her?"

"I didn't even see her!"

"Think hard. I need to know who followed her."

The kid sat with his mouth open.

"Whose room were you in?"

"Bowe's," the kid said. "Bowe Bradlee and Nic Langdon share the room."

"It looks to me like the girl is coming out of a bedroom. Do you know whose bedroom it is?"

Busby watched the video again, trying to get his bearings. "I think that would be Bowe's bedroom," he said.

Clinton nodded. This was going right where he wanted it to go. "So if it were Bradlee's bedroom, it would stand to reason that it was Bowe who followed her out. Right?"

"I guess. But I didn't see if he did or not."

"It would really help me if you did."

The kid did the open fish-mouth thing again.

Clinton decided to play a hunch. "Did you see Bradlee after this?"

Busby thought for a beat. "No. I don't remember seeing him."

"Good," Clinton said. "So if the girl came out of Bradlee's bedroom, and somebody followed her, it would stand to reason that it was Bowe who followed her, right?"

"I, uh, guess so."

"Good," Clinton said, producing a yellow legal pad and a pen. "I'm going to need you to write that down."

Chapter 26

Mo Warrick was sitting at the bar, chatting with Sarge, when Chase returned to O'Ryan's. Chase thought about running, but a life on the lam didn't appeal to him. So he walked over and sat on the stool next to Warrick.

"Hi, Mo," he said.

Mo glanced at him and then back to Sarge. "Speak of the devil." To Chase he said, "We were just discussing your bull-in-a-china-shop investigation style."

Chase feigned innocence. "Me?"

"Yeah, you. You destroyed university property and assaulted a student."

"Oh good, so the kid showed Clinton the tape?" At least something had gone right.

"He also told us you assaulted him," Warrick said. "That's two this week."

"I didn't assault him. I encouraged him to do his civic duty."

"Is that what you call it?"

"It worked, didn't it? So Clinton saw the video?"

"Yes."

"So he knows that Aley Beach left the party on her own?"

"It's not that simple, Chase," Warrick said. "It's hard to tell in the video if it was actually her, and it ends before it is certain that she wasn't followed. Add to that the ME's report that says she had sex and the preliminary DNA reports that say it was with an African-American."

Chase started to speak and Warrick held up a hand to stop him.

"The ME's report also says there is evidence of possible sexual assault."

"Rape?"

Warrick kind of shrugged. "It didn't say 'rape,' it said 'sexual assault'."

"Bowe will concede that he had sex with her." And then he remembered the way Rachel Corrigan described Bowe, which pretty much corroborated his own perception of him and said, "If he remembers her name. That doesn't mean he killed her. They have no motive."

"Clinton is going back to the university to canvass for witnesses," Warrick said. "We'll see if anyone can confirm that it is the right girl in the video and if anyone saw anyone follow her out of the room. I have to tell you, Chase, Clinton has a hard-on for this guy and so does the District Attorney. There was an alleged report of sexual assault a couple of years ago. We haven't pried the file loose from the university yet, but we will; and when we do, it's going to be the first block in a pattern of behavior that's not going to make your guy look good. If he assaulted this girl, it could give him a motive—to shut her up."

Chase thought about telling him that Rachel Corrigan saw Aley Beach later that night; but since she had thrown Aley out, she couldn't verify what happened after she left, so he kept it to himself until he could come up with a witness who saw her after that.

"Well, good luck to you then," is what he said instead.

Warrick shook his head slowly. "I don't want the kid to have done it. A kid from the streets making it out is always a good thing. I'm hoping like hell we find out he didn't do it." He stood and placed a hand on Chase's shoulder. "And you stop beating up college kids."

The city of Detroit is a patchwork of new, modern buildings interspersed with old, classical-styled buildings, mixed in with burned-out, abandoned buildings. The Wayne County Medical Examiner's office was one of the new, modern buildings, set on an expanse of green on Warren Ave. just west of Dequindere. It was actually a pretty nice-looking building, if you didn't think about all the dead bodies inside.

Chase found Tommy Chin standing on a wood crate next to a stainless-steel table. On the table lay a very large man, his internal organs visible through the hole Tommy had cut in his chest. Tommy was standing on the crate because he was only about five-two and it would have otherwise been impossible for him to see into the man's chest. He was wearing surgical scrubs, complete with matching cap and mask. The scrubs matched the avocado-green walls. Under the cap was a cowlick that refused to lie down, and under the mask was a mustache that consisted of about thirteen hairs.

Chase waited just inside the door while Tommy dictated weights and measurements into a microphone that hung next to his head. He happened to look at Chase as he lifted an oversized heart out of his patient and turned to set it in a hanging scale, like the kind found in grocery store produce departments.

Tommy dropped the heart unceremoniously into the stainless-steel receptacle that hung below the scale dial. The whole thing danced on the chain that suspended it from the ceiling." I thought I heard somewhere that you were dead," he said. "Then I saw you this morning in that lot with the dead girl, and I thought you were a fucking ghost or something."

"I'm not dead," Chase said with a laugh. "I'm retired."

"Pretty much the same thing."

"Yeah," Chase agreed, "sometimes it feels like it."

"So what's up?"

"I don't want to interrupt." He couldn't peel his eyes away from the yawning gap that the enormous heart had come from.

Tommy looked down at the body as if he had forgotten

about it. "What, this? This is nothing, just some fat slob who dropped dead from a heart attack. The widow wanted an autopsy." His chuckle was tinged with irony. "I could have told her what happened without even cutting. Look at him. The paramedics had to pry a cheeseburger out of his hand before they could work on him. But you didn't come here to talk about old Chuck, did you? You're not a friend of the family or something, are you?"

"Actually, he's my brother-in-law, my sister's fat slob of a husband."

Tommy winced. "Aw shit, Chase. I'm sorry; I didn't mean anything by that. Just blowing off some steam. It's been a long week, ya know?"

"Yeah, it's okay," Chase said. "I don't even have a sister. I was just yanking your chain."

Tommy closed his eyes and shook his head. Then he laughed. "You're an asshole."

"Yeah, but that was funny."

"Yeah, funny. What do you want? Oh, wait. Let me guess... Aley Beach."

Chase nodded. "That's right. I understand that the preliminary report says something about sexual assault?"

"*Possible* sexual assault," Tommy said. "In my opinion there's not enough to positively declare sexual assault." He looked around to ensure they were alone. "My boss was really pushing for full-blown rape. I told him I'd quit if he made me say it. He probably would have let me quit if there weren't bodies popping up all over town. So we compromised and I called it *possibl*e sexual assault."

"What's the dispute?"

"There was a small tear to the posterior fourchette. That's the point of opening in the vagina nearest the anus."

"That doesn't sound good."

"I'm sure the DA will try to use it to try and prove rape," Tommy said. "And if asked under oath if it points to rape, I would have to say it could."

"But," Chase said.

"It's not definitive. It could also be a result of rough sex or simply the size of the man."

"You mean, his, *um...* "

Tommy smiled. "Yes, his *um*."

"That can happen?"

Tommy laughed. "Never happened to you, huh?"

"No," Chase said. "Not that I know of."

"Me neither," Tommy said and laughed. "But I'm just a little Chinaman. You know what they say about us."

Chase shook his head in amusement. Tommy was a trip. "But with a six-ten black man?"

Tommy nodded, turning serious. "You don't even have to play into the stereotype; if his *um* is proportional to the rest of him, I'd say it is a very real possibility that it occurred during consensual sex."

Chase nodded. That was good. If Tommy would testify to it, they could take the rape motive off the table. "Let me ask you something else, Tommy."

"Shoot."

"You said Aley was strangled manually. Wouldn't that take a lot of force?"

Tommy nodded. "To an extent," he said. "It would also help if the perp had big hands and a lot of strength, as I imagine our six-ten hypothetical friend did. But someone smaller and weaker could do it if they were determined and/or got lucky and just happened to grasp the neck in a position to compress the larynx and obstruct the airway."

Chase thought back to the adrenaline that rushed through his veins when he kicked in the door to Aley's dorm room. "Or if they had a rush of adrenaline?"

"Adrenaline is a remarkable thing. It can definitely give a person strength that they wouldn't ordinarily have."

"So it doesn't necessarily take a big, strong person to

strangle someone," Chase said.

"No," Tommy agreed. "But it helps."

"How long would it take for the person being strangled to die?"

"The brain generally dies after being deprived of oxygen for about three minutes."

Three minutes? Holy shit! "So the person doing the strangling has to be really committed to it."

Tommy nodded. "Yes, unless they managed to crush the larynx and obstruct the airway, then the person wouldn't have to hold onto it for three minutes, but it would still take three minutes for death to occur."

"Okay," Chase said. "Three minutes is a long-ass time. Nobody is just going to lie there and let themselves be choked for three minutes. She would have fought like hell, scratching, hitting and kicking. Was there any DNA under her nails?"

Tommy smiled. "You're good, Chase. I guess you haven't been out of the game too long after all. Yes, she had some skin tissue, not her own, under her fingernails."

"And?"

Tommy shrugged.

"What's that mean?"

"It means I don't know. The scrapings were taken from me. I assume they're being tested, but you'd have to ask my boss."

Chapter 27

Chase drove back to O'Ryan's thinking about the case. On the one hand, he was pretty sure that a good defense lawyer could explain away all of the physical evidence and get Bowe an acquittal. On the other hand, he was sure that Howard Frazier didn't have an acquittal in mind. And he didn't really want to deal with Kendrick Martin when Frazier said, "Sic 'im."

It made sense though. No team was going to waste a pick, let alone the first pick, on a guy who had a murder indictment hanging over him; there's literally millions of dollars at stake. Chase was pretty sure that Bowe was innocent, but there was enough physical evidence for Clinton and the DA to get an indictment. What a cluster this was turning out to be.

He was cruising down Woodward while these thoughts ran through his mind. He wasn't paying attention to what was going on around him; he should have been.

Woodward is five lanes. Two lanes going in each direction with a left turn lane down the center. Chase was in the right- hand lane heading south. Out of the corner of his eye, he saw a beater sedan of some sort creeping up in the next lane. A beater in Detroit is not cause for alarm, but the two guys in the car were. They wore black bandanas around the lower halves of their faces, like Frank and Jesse James, with black sunglasses and black baseball caps screwed on sideways. A quick look in the rearview mirror confirmed an identical pair of gangbangers following in another beater. They had timed it perfectly. He was boxed in by the two cars and parked cars to the right.

"Shit," Chase said to himself.

By the time he looked back to the left, the car on the side

had pulled up even and the passenger had an assault rifle pointed at him. He said "Shit!" again. For some reason the scene from *Top Gun* when Tom Cruise says, "I'm going to hit the brakes, and he'll fly right by," popped into Chase's head. So he stomped on the brakes. The tires screamed as they bit into pavement. A fraction of a second later, the assault rifle chattered a stream of bullets that punched a line of holes into the Charger's hood.

Another fraction of a second after that, the trailing car slammed into Chase's rear bumper. There is no sound on Earth like the sickening crunch of metal striking metal as two cars collide. The airbag exploded open, whacking Chase in the face; and the rear window shattered, peppering him from behind with small bits of tempered safety glass like shotgun pellets.

The car to the left roared and sped away as Chase's car bounced off of two parked cars and spun to a stop, facing the car that had rear-ended him. Nothing happened for a second. After all the commotion, it was eerily quiet; then a bullet punched through the windshield. Chase ducked behind the dash as best he could and pushed the airbag out of his face while pulling his Beretta. A hail of bullets finished off the windshield and tore up the front seats. Chase waited, somewhat impatiently, for a break in the salvo. It finally stopped and he popped up, pointed through the missing windshield and squeezed off the entire clip. Then he dropped back down and awaited return fire while ejecting the spent clip and replacing it with a full one. He waited several seconds and no return fire came, so he slowly rose to peek over the dashboard. Nothing moved.

The body of the Charger had been crumpled. Chase had to kick the door to get it open. The driver of the other car was slumped in his seat. The driver's side window was covered with plastic. One corner hung loose. Chase pulled the rest of the plastic loose. Blood soaked the bandana wrapped around the kid's face. He had a hole in his forehead. It had either been a lucky shot or an unlucky shot, depending on one's perspective. The sunglasses that Chase had seen the driver wearing prior to the crash were nowhere in sight; his eyes were open but sightless. Chase grasped the bandana and pulled it down past the driver's chin... Gerald Robinson. Chase sighed, not happy at all with having killed the kid, even if he had been a drug dealer intent on killing him.

The other banger, dressed in the same Old West bank-robber outfit, lay on the sidewalk in front of a cell-phone store. Chase figured he had been hanging out the passenger window to fire when their car had rear-ended his. The abrupt stop had thrown him from the car. He wasn't dead, but he was certainly going to feel it in the morning. Chase used his foot to roll the kid over. Half his face had been scraped away, but it was the same kid who he had pistol-whipped the night he had shot out the window of the car. The kid was having a tough week. He moaned as blood seeped from the road rash.

Chase picked up a machine pistol that looked just like the ones he had taken from the other BD Boyz. He wanted to secure it in the trunk of his Charger, but the trunk was almost in the back seat and wouldn't open. So he ejected the clip and stuck it under the driver's seat. He threw the rest of the gun in the back seat. He then stuck his head in the cell-phone store and asked the clerk to call 911.

Chapter 28

It took a full twenty minutes for an ambulance to arrive. The paramedics pronounced the gangbanger driver dead. They scraped the other kid off the sidewalk and rushed him to the hospital. Twenty minutes later two patrol cars arrived. The owner of the cell-phone store had spent the time trying to get Chase to upgrade his phone. Chase finally broke free of him and walked out to meet the cops.

"We were dispatched to a traffic accident," the driver of the first patrol car said, surveying the scene and taking charge. He was a couple of inches shorter than Chase and several years younger. He wore body armor under his dark-blue uniform shirt. The name tag said "Baker." Chase had heard stories about the eyes of soldiers in combat; they called it a "thousand-yard stare." This kid had eyes that Chase imagined the thousand-yard stare looked like.

"I guess you could call it that."

Baker looked at the two cars that had been transformed into accordions. "What would you call it?"

"Attempted murder?"

Baker looked skeptical, like he thought Chase was exaggerating. His partner called out to him from where he inspected the hood of Chase's Charger. "Hey, Bake, these look like bullet holes."

"We got a body over here, Bake," the driver of the second patrol car said, looking through the driver's window of the gangbangers' car. "Looks like he was shot."

There are somewhere between 3,500 and 5,000 police officers in Detroit, depending on which report or newspaper you read. So it wasn't too much of a stretch for these four guys to not know who Chase was. Apparently, his career hadn't been as distinguished as he had thought. He thought briefly about playing the do-you-know-who-I-am card, but thought better of it. He'd be ahead of the game if they just didn't shoot him.

It wouldn't have done any good anyway; Baker wasn't taking any chances. He threw Chase against the wrecked Charger, frisked him, handcuffed him and secured him in the back of one of the patrol cars.

Chase sat there for at least another twenty minutes, watching the officers cordon off the area around the cars and direct traffic around the scene until the detectives arrived. It was not comfortable sitting in the back of the patrol car with his hands cuffed behind his back, and the longer he sat there, the stiffer he became. The stiffer and sorer he got, the more annoyed he became.

Detectives surveyed the scene and listened to reports from the patrol cops. There was a lot of pointing and looking around. They came into a huddle and then broke apart to point and look some more. At one point Baker pointed at Chase. Chase tried to snarl to show his displeasure. Fortunately, or maybe unfortunately, the detective that Baker pointed Chase out to knew him. His name was Luther Farrow. When Luther saw who was in the back of the patrol car, he broke out in a hearty laugh.

"Fuck you, Luther!" Chase yelled through the closed window. "Get me out of here."

Luther Farrow wore a brown leather trench coat and matching fedora. He couldn't have been more stereotypical black Detroit police detective if he'd tried. He smiled, showing big teeth stained by the cigars he smoked, and held his hand to his ear as if he couldn't hear Chase through the glass.

"Open the fucking door, Luther!" Chase shouted.

He did, after another round of laughter. "Hey, Denzel," he said. "What's happenin'?"

"I'm glad you're enjoying this, Luther."

"Oh, I am, Chase. I truly am enjoying this."

"Get me out of here."

"In a minute, but first tell me what happened."

Chase told Luther about being boxed in by the two beaters and slamming on his brakes, causing the crash that saved his life.

Luther's eyebrows pinched together in a scowl. "So two cars of gangbangers just arbitrarily picked *you* out of all the *thousands* of people in Detroit and shot up your car?"

"They were trying to shoot *me,* " Chase said. "And I didn't say it was arbitrary."

"What'd you do to provoke them?"

"It's a long story."

"We'll get to the long story later. Just give me the highlights."

Chase pointed to Gerald Robinson still in the driver's seat of the wrecked beater. "I extricated a young man from the employ of that one—"

"Drug dealer?"

Chase nodded. "Yeah, and I might have pistol-whipped the one who was taken to the hospital."

Luther laughed. "That sounds like you. Anything else?"

"I hit Atari Black in the mouth with the butt end of a shotgun."

That bit of information sent Farrow to laughing so hard he had to bend over and put his hands on his knees to keep from falling over in the street. "Damn, Chase!" he said when he finally got himself under control. "You are one dumb-ass white boy."

Chase didn't think it was funny at all and hadn't uttered a single *ha*. "Whatever. Just get me out of here."

"Hold on a minute," Farrow said and shut the door in Chase's face.

Chase yelled for him again, but he didn't come back. It

wasn't his fault that Chase was in the position he was in, but he still cussed Farrow out even if he couldn't hear him.

One of the guys from the medical examiner's office pulled Gerald Robinson out of the car and zipped him up in a black body bag. A CSU team had arrived. They searched the area for spent shells, putting numbered yellow tents over each one they found. Chase stopped counting at twenty-two.

Farrow finally came back and pulled Chase from the car. He uncuffed him and told him he was free to go. "You need to come down to the station to give a statement. Your car will be towed to the impound lot and examined for evidence. We'll let you know when you can pick it up."

"Why? So I can have it towed to a junkyard?"

"You've got insurance, don't you?"

"Not much. Do you know how much it costs to insure a car in Detroit?"

Farrow nodded gravely. "Unfortunately, I do."

Chase paid his last respects to his Charger. He had loved that car. It was a piece of shit; but he had been comfortable in it, and it had taken a bullet—several bullets actually—to save his life.

"By the way," Farrow said, "Sergeant Clinton told me to tell you that he will have your ass if he finds you snooping around in his case again."

Chase told Farrow what he could tell Sergeant Clinton to do to himself and then started to walk down Woodward. Farrow's laugh followed.

Chapter 29

Chase took a cab back to D State to visit again with Dennis Harden. The ride gave him time to regain his composure after a second near-death experience in as many days. By the time the cab dropped him in front of the small station house, he had already stiffened up from the small of his back all the way to the base of his skull. He felt like he was wearing a body cast.

"Aley Beach."

"The dead girl," Harden said.

"The drug dealer," Chase said.

"Get outta here. She was dealing?"

Chase was pissed. "What? A little white girl from the sticks can't be a Detroit drug dealer?"

Harden shook his head in disbelief. "I never would have guessed it."

"Me neither."

"Did you take this to the DPD?"

"The DPD doesn't want to know that their victim was a drug dealer. It might open their case to possibilities other than Bowe."

"I was never a big-shot detective like you, but that seems about right. Grab onto a suspect and hold on as long as you can, especially if it's a high-profile suspect who will get your name in the papers."

"I need to know about the previous rape allegation, Dennis," Chase said.

Harden scowled and shook his head. "Never happened."

"Really? You're sure?"

"If the number-one college basketball player in the country raped someone on my campus, I would know about it."

"Was he ever accused?"

Harden folded his arms across his chest. "Accused? Yes. But the girl recanted. Told me she had had too much to drink the night in question and couldn't remember exactly what had happened."

"So why did she think she had been raped?"

Harden shook his head. "You'd have to ask her."

"And you'll give me her name?"

"Sure, Chase. Anything for you."

Chase nodded. "Can I ask you one more question?"

Harden sighed. "Absolutely, I'm here to serve," he said, dripping with sarcasm.

"If the number-one basketball player in the country *had* raped someone, there might be those who would want to cover it up. How can I know that you're not on the take?" Harden exploded from his chair. "Man, get the fuck outta my office before I bust a cap in your ass."

Chase laughed all the way across the office and winked at the desk cop. "Don't forget, Dennis," he said, "you lost the bet."

"Janay," Harden yelled to the desk cop from his office door, "if you see this man again, shoot him."

Chase cabbed it again back to O'Ryan's. He tried to block out the aching in his back and think about the case. He still had no idea who had killed Aley Beach and dumped her body. He was sure it hadn't been Bowe, but it was clear that he would have to find out who did if he wanted to clear him. Unfortunately, he didn't even have a suspect, let alone evidence.

The black Escalade was parked in front of the bar with the crazy, violent ex-offensive tackle standing next to it. Sometimes it's just not your day.

"Howard wants to talk to you," Kendrick said.

"Wonderful."

Kendrick raised one eyebrow. Chase imagined it was the same look he had under his helmet as he tried to figure out his duties on whatever play had been called. "Are you going to be a problem?"

"No," Chase said. He didn't have the energy to fight, and he sure as hell wasn't interested in getting bounced off the sidewalk.

Kendrick opened the back door, and Chase climbed carefully in under his own power. Howard Frazier sat in the same seat wearing all black again. There was a smart-ass comment in there somewhere, but again Chase didn't have the energy.

Frazier noticed the way Chase climbed in and sat gingerly. "What's wrong with you?"

Chase relaxed into the soft leather seat. "Nothing. Did you want something? Or were you looking for fashion tips?" Apparently, he did have the energy.

Frazier sighed loudly like a parent unhappy with his child and not sure how to deal with him. "The word going around is that they're going to convene a grand jury and try to indict Bowe for the murder of that girl."

"I heard."

Howard turned about forty-five degrees and looked menacingly at Chase. "I thought we had talked about this," he said. "We *cannot* afford to have him indicted."

"I know."

"Well, what are you doing about it?"

"I'm working on it."

"Work harder."

"All right. Relax," Chase said. "Let me ask you something. What happened with the prior sexual-assault allegation?"

Frazier was taken aback. Chase wasn't sure if it were because he told him to relax or if it were because of the question. Frazier took a moment to get his composure back

163

and then said, "What do you mean?"

"Were the charges dropped?"

"He was never charged."

"Why?"

"What do you mean 'why'?"

"Why wasn't he charged? Lack of evidence? Or did you pay someone off?"

"I really don't see what that has to do with—"

"If it were lack of evidence," Chase said, "Bowe might have thought he wouldn't get lucky twice. If you paid somebody off, then he would know that you would do it again."

Chase could see that Frazier didn't want to implicate himself. He didn't blame him. "Again," Frazier said, "what does it have to do with—"

"The first way, he might have killed her to keep her from accusing him again. The second way, he wouldn't have."

Frazier didn't speak. An internal struggle raged within him. Does he protect himself or his meal ticket?

Chase let him sweat for a second and then said, "Or maybe it's neither. Maybe you had Kendrick kill the girl. That way you wouldn't have to pay anybody off this time. Save a little money for another of those fine black suits."

"I did not have Kendrick or anybody else, for that matter, kill that girl."

"Because you knew you could get any charges dropped. You can buy anything in this town, can't you?"

Frazier struggled again for a moment before finally saying, "Yes, you can. *If* you were inclined to do something like that and there was a willing seller."

It was a good answer. He had told Chase that he had paid someone off the previous time and could do it again, if necessary, without actually saying it.

"So why don't you just buy his way out this time?"

"Like I said, there has to be a willing seller."

"Clinton?"

"Racist motherfucker," Frazier mumbled.

Frazier was the most racist person Chase had ever met, but he let it go. It wouldn't do any good to argue the point. He would have been proud of Clinton for not taking the bribe, if the reason he had turned it down was noble and not the fact that he wanted to hang the murder on Bowe.

"I'll take care of Clinton," Chase said. "There's no way he'll get a conviction."

"We already discussed this," Frazier said in that exasperated parent tone. "You remember? The LSU football player? Bowe can't even be associated with this if he's going to go number one."

"I forgot," Chase said. "It's all about the money."

Frazier smiled. "Son, *everything* is about the money."

"Well, hell. I thought it was about saving the kid."

Frazier nodded and for just a second turned into a human being. "That too," he said. "He's a good kid, and I don't believe he did it."

"I don't either," Chase said.

But who the hell did?

Chapter 30

Jason Gardner, one of the usual drunks, blasted through the heavy door of O'Ryan's, nearly knocking Chase into the street.

"Hey, Jason," Chase said. "Where's the fire?"

Gardner stopped and looked at Chase, startled. "Oh, hey, Chase."

"Everything okay?"

"Yes, fine," Gardner said and took off down the street, looking over his shoulder twice to see if he were being followed.

Strange. Chase entered O'Ryan's to find Mo Warrick sitting at the bar, lost in thought. He was in full assistant chief uniform. The four stars that adorned each side of his jacket collar caught the light and twinkled like stars in the sky. A cup of coffee sat on the bar in front of him.

"Is there a parade today?" Chase said, mounting the stool next to his.

Warrick looked at Chase out of the corner of his eye. "Shut up," he said and took a sip from the coffee.

"Okay."

"You've had an exciting few days." It wasn't a question.

"I don't know if I'd say—"

"Shut up." He emphasized it this time. So Chase shut up. "Roughing up a college kid is one thing," Warrick continued, "but shooting up Woodward is something else entirely. The chief wants me to rein you in."

Chase had never been a fan of being reprimanded; he didn't handle it well. It was one of the things that had kept him doing the one-step-forward, two-steps-back thing while he had been with the department. "With all due respect, Mo, I don't work for the chief anymore."

"But I do," Warrick countered. "He wants me to 'throw your white ass in the county jail.' That was a direct quote, by the way. How many guys in there do you think are down with the BD Boyz?"

"I was defending myself."

Warrick shook his head. "That don't matter. You went and stirred up a whole shit storm. You are responsible for the fall-out."

"*I'm* responsible?"

"Yes, *you* are responsible."

"Why am I responsible?"

"Because I said so!" Warrick said, slamming his hand down on the counter.

Chase laughed; he couldn't help himself. "Feel better?"

Warrick smiled and shook his head, taking a deep breath. "Shit, Chase. The DA went to the chief and complained about you. And she said I had 'encouraged' you, so the chief chewed my ass out."

"Don't worry, Mo," Chase said, "you still have plenty of ass. He probably did you a favor. You've been sitting behind that desk too long."

"Remind me to tell you to go fuck yourself the next time you come sniffing around. In the meantime, where are you on the Bowe Bradlee stuff?"

"He didn't do it."

"Do you have evidence?"

"Sort of."

Warrick chuckled and said, "sort of" under his breath. "I can't take 'sort of' to the DA."

"I need time. I'm working solo here."

"Time's running out, Chase. They've got witnesses that put Bowe and the dead girl together. They've got enough physical evidence to prove sexual assault; it's thin, but they can make the case. And nobody saw the girl after the party."

"Nobody?"

Warrick shook his head. "Clinton knocked on every door in the dorm. Not only did nobody see her; he has a witness who says he was in the lobby all night and swears she never returned."

"Well, I beg to differ," Chase said, thinking about Rachel Corrigan at home in Port Huron. "I have a witness who can put Aley in *her* dorm room *after* the party."

"And Aley stayed in the dorm all night?"

"Well, no. They had an argument and Aley left."

"So it's possible that she went back to Bowe, or Bowe came to her."

"Whose side are you on?" Chase said.

"Do you know how much easier my life would be if I just threw you in jail and let the DA indict the kid? Don't give me that whose-side-are-you-on bullshit. The DA is in the process of convening a grand jury. She will have it in a few days, and she *will* get an indictment."

"Shit."

"Yeah, shit," Warrick said. "You need to find someone who can tell us how that girl ended up dead in that lot."

The outside door opened. Another of the regular drunks stepped in, saw Warrick and stepped back out.

"You're killing my business," Chase said.

"Right back at'cha, pal."

Chase spent the rest of the evening in O'Ryan's with Sally. She was quiet and avoided any conversation about anything of significance. He respected that, and they spent most of the night not talking. The silence between them was deafening. They closed at 2 a.m. and Chase hit the street, headed back to the D State campus.

There was no way that Clinton had talked to *everybody* in the dorm. He didn't have that sort of work ethic. It also might have ruined his case against Bowe.

Chase stood outside the dorm for about twenty minutes, freezing his ass off. It didn't matter how warm it got during the day; as soon as the sun went down, it got cold. Nobody had come or gone from the dorm. It was either the cold, or the fact that it was a school night or they were avoiding the guy who looked like a cop standing outside the dorm.

A few kids walked past and either told him to get lost or circled around far enough to avoid his approach. A bus stopped at the end of the block. A lone figure got off and headed toward the dorm, her hands jammed into the pockets of the parka she wore. Her head was burrowed down into the turned-up collar. Her hair was in braids pulled tightly to her scalp. Peeking out from the collar of the parka was perfect, mocha-colored skin and a pair of the most beautiful, deep-brown eyes Chase had ever seen.

"Excuse me," he said as she neared.

"No," she said, not looking at him.

"No what?"

"No whatever. I'm not interested. I don't have any money. I already know Jesus. And I have mace in my hand right now. Want to see it?"

Chase took a step back and held his hands up in a defensive posture. "Whoa, easy. I'm not here for any of that. I'm just looking for information. Did you hear about the girl who lived in this building and got killed?"

"No." She tried to push past. Chase stepped into her path.

"Are you sure? Her name was Aley Beach."

She finally stopped. Her face popped out of the parka. It was as beautiful as her eyes. She looked at Chase, disbelief in those incredible dark-brown eyes. "She's dead? I heard something about her taking off or dropping out or something. She's dead?"

"Yes. She was last seen leaving her room at about this time. I'm hoping to find somebody who is normally out here about now."

"Well, you found one. I work over at the MGM Grand, serving drinks in the casino. I get off at 2 a.m."

"My name is Chase."

"Merlene."

"Merlene," Chase said, "Aley disappeared the night the basketball team won their conference tournament. Do you remember that night?"

Merlene nodded. "People were acting like fools all over campus that night."

"Did you work that night?"

"Mmm-hmm."

"Did you happen to see Aley out here on your way home?"

Merlene thought for a few seconds. "Now that you mention it, I did see her that night. I remember she was crying and wasn't wearing a coat. All she had on was a skirt and a top."

Chase let out the breath he had been holding. Could this be the break he had been looking for? "Do you remember where she went?"

"She got into a pickup truck, a big black thing, with long red antennas and Confederate flag stickers in the back window."

"You're sure?" What are the chances that there were two trucks like that?

Merlene scowled. "You think I'm going to forget something like that?"

Chase smiled, feeling like a boob. "I guess not." He thanked Merlene and stepped aside, letting her enter the dorm. He watched her enter safely inside and then turned his attention back to the black truck. "That son of a bitch," he said to himself.

Chapter 31

Chase couldn't go wandering around in the middle of the night, looking for Dan Gentry. The kid was probably asleep anyway, so Chase went home and slept too, though not very well. His mind wouldn't stop racing. Did it all lead back to Emerson after all? He had gotten bad vibes there, and it wasn't just when his face was bouncing off the cell bars. Bunch of racist hicks.

When he awoke, the sun was shining and the morning frost had melted. It was later than he had wanted to get started, but what are you going do? He was tired.

Chase borrowed Sarge's truck since his Charger looked like Bonnie and Clyde's getaway car. It was a Ford F250 and drove like a tank. Why did Sarge need to drive a tank anyway? It wasn't like he was a big off-roader or hunter or had much of anything to do with the outdoors. Maybe he was compensating for something? Chase filed it away in the back of his head to ask Sarge about it when he got back to the city.

He made good time. Sleeping late got him around the bulk of the morning rush hour, and he rolled into downtown Emerson at about the same time he would have if he had left at the crack of dawn. He slid under the blinking yellow light in the center of town, keeping his eyes peeled for a patrol car. If anybody were actually keeping an eye out for him, they'd be looking for a black Charger, not a big-ass mint-green F250. Hell, now that he thought about it, the truck was the perfect disguise.

The dirt road that the Beaches lived on was mud in the early spring. Chase wheeled through the muck and slop, glad to be driving the big truck. Maybe this pick-up truck thing wasn't such a bad idea, although Chase didn't think that Sarge drove on any dirt roads.

He turned into the Beaches' driveway and pulled to a stop near the house. Gentry's big black beater was there. Chase hoped Gentry was as well.

John Beach stepped from the barn. He wore blue denim overalls and held a pitchfork in his hand, a la American Gothic. He studied the truck, trying to determine who had driven onto his property.

Chase climbed from the truck and shut the door. The side was completely covered in mud. He wished he had a pair of knee-high rubber boots like Beach.

The screen door squealed, and Mrs. Beach stepped out onto the porch. "Detective Chase," she said. "I didn't expect you." She looked like she hadn't slept since the last time Chase had seen her.

Chase started to speak but was cut off by John Beach.

"He's not a detective, Tracy," Beach said. "Go call Bradshaw at the Sheriff's department."

Chase looked at Beach. He still held the pitchfork. Chase moved his hand slowly to the Beretta on his hip.

Tracy Beach looked at her husband and then back to Chase. "You're not?"

"I never actually said I was," Chase said. He knew how lame it was as soon as it passed his lips. He shook my head. "Okay, look—"

"He's working for the nigger," Beach said.

"You mean…" his wife said. Her left arm was around her chest. Her right hand rested on her left shoulder. It was as if she were hugging herself for comfort.

"Yes, Tracy, the nigger that killed her," Beach said.

"Wait a minute," Chase said. "I am not working for Bowe. I'm looking into the matter as a favor to a friend."

"And who might that be?" Beach said.

Chase sighed. "Bowe's high school coach."

Beach snorted. "Go call Bradshaw," he again told his wife.

"Okay, I know what it looks like," Chase said. "But please, listen to me for one minute." He looked back and forth between the husband and wife. Neither stopped him, so he continued. "I have dug up witnesses that saw Aley *after* the party... without Bowe."

Beach didn't believe him. "Why didn't Sergeant Clinton tell us this?"

"Because he has his suspect, and he isn't looking for any evidence that he can't use to convict him. *I'm* looking for the truth."

"And if the truth is that the nigger raped and killed her?"

"Then I will turn my evidence over to Clinton. But I really don't think Bowe did it." Again, neither of the Beaches stopped him so he continued, "I actually have a witness who saw Aley getting into a big, black pick-up truck with long red antennas and Confederate flag stickers in the back window."

It took a moment for what Chase had said to sink in, and then both of the Beaches looked at the big, black pick-up truck with long red antennas and Confederate flag stickers in the back window parked in their driveway.

John Beach was the first to react. "That son of a bitch," he said. He turned and marched back toward the barn, screaming Gentry's name.

Tracy Beach still hugged herself. "Not Dan," she moaned as Chase took up pursuit of her husband.

Chase entered the barn seconds after Beach. Beach had Dan Gentry pinned to the wall of a horse stall with the pitchfork pressed to his chest. The tines of the fork indented the material of Gentry's Carhartt jacket. They didn't appear to have pierced it... yet. Gentry looked terrified. He didn't have a clue as to what was going on or why his employer was on the verge of running him through with a pitchfork. His eyes goggled and searched desperately for help.

"Did you kill my daughter?" Beach said.

"What? No. I—"

"Don't lie to me!"

"Who told you that?"

"I did," Chase said, stopping just behind Beach's shoulder.

Gentry looked at Chase and blanched. "What did you tell him?"

"A witness saw Aley getting into your truck the night she disappeared."

The kid deflated like a balloon. Had Beach popped him with the pitchfork? "I can explain," he said, defeated.

"You can explain?" Beach said. "You can explain why my daughter was in your truck and you forgot to mention that to me?" He leaned harder on the pitchfork.

"John!" Tracy Beach had entered the barn, looking as defeated as Gentry. "Stop, John," she said. "Put the pitchfork down and let him explain."

It took a beat for her words to pierce the shroud of anger that encircled Beach's mind. Eventually he withdrew the pitchfork from the young man's chest and then raised it slightly and thrust it into the ground less than an inch from Gentry's foot. "Talk."

Chapter 32

"I was home watching TV the night Aley disappeared," Gentry said.

It sounded a little far-fetched, but Chase let it go. Beach didn't.

"At 2:30 a.m.," he said, "when you had to be to work in just a few hours?"

Gentry looked back and forth from Beach to Chase. Chase nodded. "Go on."

"She was crying," Gentry said, "and asked me to come and get her. It was an hour's drive, and it was the middle of the night; but she begged me, so I went."

He paused to assess. So far so good, so he continued, "She burst through the door as soon as I pulled up to the dorm."

"What was she wearing?" Chase said.

Gentry thought for a second. "Um, a short black skirt and a tight-fitting white blouse."

"What about a coat?"

"No."

He had it right so far. "Okay, go on."

"Her makeup was a mess from all the crying, and her hair was messed up. I asked her if she was okay, and she said she was.

"She climbed up into the cab of the truck and scooted to the center of the bench seat like she used to when we were in high school. I asked her if she wanted to talk about whatever had happened, and she said that she didn't right then.

"She turned on the radio and we just drove around for a while until we came to a park in Gross Pointe, I think it was. I'm not real familiar with that area."

"That's fine," Chase said. "Go on."

Gentry snuck a peek at the pitchfork and took a deep

175

breath. "I parked facing the Detroit River and cut the headlights. It was a clear night, and the moon reflected off the river. I have to admit, I was happy that she had called. I hoped we'd get back together."

"You had broken up?" Beach said. The father is always the last to know these things.

"Um, yes, sir," Gentry said and flinched.

"Go on," Mrs. Beach said. Chase had forgotten that she was there. She still stood just inside the barn. She still hugged herself and looked to be on the verge of a breakdown as Gentry described the last night of her daughter's life.

"She told me that she had made a mess of things," Gentry said. "I said something like it couldn't be that bad, but she said it was. I feel bad now, but I was kind of happy at the time. You know, because she had left me and it had gone bad for her. I know it sounds selfish, but... well, anyway, I thought she'd come back home. But she said she couldn't. That she'd made such a big deal about going off to college in the city, and she didn't want to look like a failure."

He paused again to reassess, to see if Beach were going to pick up the pitchfork. Then he continued, "I didn't know what to say, so we just sat there for a while, listening to the radio and looking at the river. After a while, I thought she had fallen asleep, but then she asked me to take her back to her dorm. I tried again to get her to come home with me, but she wouldn't. She said she had to get her act together. That's when I knew."

"Knew what?" Beach said.

"That she wasn't my Aley anymore. She had changed."

Beach nodded. It was the same thing he had said to Chase in his daughter's bedroom.

"So I took her back and dropped her off," Gentry said.

Beach leaned on the pitchfork. His back was to Chase so he couldn't see his face, but his breathing was deep and labored.

"So you took her back and just drove away?" Chase said.

Gentry nodded. "I watched her go back into the dorm before I left."

"I heard you were pretty upset about Aley's spending time with other guys at school. It's hard to believe you would have just let her walk away."

Gentry nodded and looked ashamed. "I was angry, but there was something about her that night. Like I said, she wasn't my Aley anymore. She had changed. I felt it, and I just... knew that she and I were through for good."

"You didn't think to tell us about this?" Beach said.

"I don't know. I mean, my head knew that me and Aley were through, but I guess I hadn't really believed it yet. It took a while to really sink in. Ya know?" He nodded his head as if to help Beach understand.

"No, I don't know," Beach said.

"I get it," Mrs. Beach said.

Beach turned to his wife. "What? What do you mean, 'you get' it?"

Mrs. Beach walked to her husband and gently grasped the shoulder strap of his overalls. "I understand what he's saying. I guess I can't really explain it either, but I understand. Sometimes it takes a while for your heart to catch up with your head."

"Well, I don't 'get it' at all," Beach said.

"I know," she said softly.

"Let's go back to that night," Chase said. "Did you see anything? A person, a car, anything or anybody who might have been waiting for her or just didn't look right?"

Gentry shook his head. "No. Like I said, she went into the dorm and disappeared. She should have been safe once she was inside."

"Yes," Chase said, "she should have been."

Clinton sat in the Frank Murphy Hall of Justice and tried

not to scoff. Hall of Justice—yeah, right. Unless you're connected to the city council or mayor or any of their underlings or bribers, then you were golden. As much as he hated Chase, he respected the fact that he went after that council lady's kid. And look what it got him… fired. Clinton couldn't wait to get out of this city.

"What have you got, Andy?" the punk kid assistant prosecutor said; disrespect dripped off of him.

Clinton was pissed that he had been sent to this kid who looked like he had graduated from high school last week instead of the homicide division chief. He wanted to drop-kick the darky across the room and shove his bow tie up his ass. Who did this kid think he was? Clinton had been busting heads on the street when this kid had been drinking Kool-Aid and watching Bugs Bunny and shitting himself. And he was going to look down his nose at Clinton?

"Well, boy," Clinton said, "what I've got is the presumptive number-one pick in the NBA draft locked up on a murder charge. Do you think you can handle that? Or should we call in your babysitter?"

"Wait a minute," the kid said. "You've got evidence that pins a murder on Bowe Bradlee?"

Clinton crossed his arms over his chest and nodded.

"What's the evidence?"

"You know what?" Clinton said, "I changed my mind. Fuck you. I'm not giving my evidence to some snot-nosed kid fresh out of whatever night-school college you went to. This is the big time, son. Get me the DA herself."

Chapter 33

Back to Port Huron. Chase was already halfway there as the crow flies. Unfortunately, he wasn't a crow, and it took almost as long to navigate his way back to the highway and onto Port Huron as it would have if he had driven straight there from Detroit.

He drove straight to the "Happy Days" house. The driveway was empty, and the house felt empty as well. He knocked on the door and confirmed the feeling... nobody was home.

It was a little past noon and Chase was hungry—might as well eat while he waited. He found a café on the waterfront and ordered a burger. A freighter slid slowly past, headed north. He wasn't sure if it were full or empty, which seemed fitting since at that moment he felt as if he didn't know anything at all. First, Aley Beach had been at the party, and then she wasn't. Then she had been in her dorm room, and then she wasn't. Then she was in her ex-boyfriend's truck, and then she wasn't. Then she was going back into the dorm, and then what? This case was bouncing around like a racquetball.

The waitress who served the burger was about the same age as Rachel Corrigan. Chase asked if she might happen to know Rachel, and she said, "No." Of course not... another swing and miss.

Chase finished off the food without really tasting it and drove back to Rachel Corrigan's house. He parked at the curb across the street. He didn't know what else to do. He sure as hell wasn't going to find her by driving around a city that he didn't know, even if he called her name out the window. She'd be back eventually. Chase just hoped it wouldn't be too long. He hated stakeouts.

It wasn't long before an all-black patrol car with red and blue roof lights eased to a stop at the curb behind him. A female officer stepped out of the car. Her pants and uniform shirt were a dark blue, almost as dark as her car. Her hair was straw blonde, slicked back into a ponytail. Her right hand rested on the butt of the automatic she wore on her hip.

She walked with the same self-assured swagger cops world-wide walk with. "License, registration and proof of insurance, please," she said when she reached the truck.

"Is there a problem?" Chase said.

"License, registration and proof of insurance, please," she repeated.

Chase thought about turning on the charm, but this lady looked immune to charm, and he didn't really have any anyway. "Okay. Let me see what I can find. This isn't my truck. I borrowed it from a friend." He rummaged in the glove box and came up with a rumpled registration and a proof-of-insurance card with the printing distorted by water marks. He handed them out the window with a smile.

The officer took them from his hand. "Driver's license, please."

Chase got it out of his wallet and passed it over. "Is there a problem?" he said again.

"The license and registration don't match," The lady said with the personality of Robocop.

"I just said I borrowed the truck from a friend."

Her hand returned to her hip. "Why don't you put your hands on the steering wheel where I can see them?"

Chase sighed and did as instructed. "Look, Officer... Charles," he said, reading the name on the nameplate affixed to her shirt, "I'm not sure what the problem is, but you can call the Detroit Police Department. They will confirm my identity and the identity of the truck's owner. We are both retired from the DPD."

He couldn't read her expression because she didn't have

one. He expected her to return to her car and run him through the system, but she just stood there looking at him. "We got a call from a homeowner. She was suspicious of a man sitting in a truck, looking suspicious—so what are you doing?"

"I'm waiting for the young lady who lives in the house across the street. I'm investigating a murder down in the city, and I need to ask her a couple of questions."

"You just said you're retired."

This lady was impossible, but Chase held his cool. His plan was to ask Rachel Corrigan a few questions and then get the hell out of there. The last thing he needed was another night in jail. "I guess I did," he said. "I suppose this would be considered an unofficial investigation."

Just then a bright-yellow VW Beatle pulled to a stop at the curb across the street. Rachel Corrigan exited the car and looked at them curiously. She turned to walk up the driveway.

"Rachel," Chase called.

Rachel turned back and took a step in their direction, trying to make out who had called out her name.

"It's me, Chase."

"Mr. Chase?" she said, walking toward the truck.

"Do you know this gentleman?" Officer Charles said.

"Yes. I've talked to him a couple of times. He's investigating my roommate's death."

"He says he has a couple of questions for you."

"Really?" Rachel said to Chase. "I swear I already told you everything I know."

"I've come across some new information, Rachel. We need to talk."

"Do you want to answer his questions?" Officer Charles said.

"I guess so."

"Okay, go ahead," the police officer told Chase. He started to open the door, and Officer Charles pushed it shut.

"Just stay where you are."

"But, I—"

"I am not leaving you alone with this young lady. If you want to ask questions, you go right ahead."

It was clear that Robocop wasn't going to leave, so Chase bit his tongue again. "Rachel," he said, "after Aley left the dorm that night, she was picked up by her boyfriend."

"AJ?"

"What? AJ? AJ Who?"

"AJ Harris."

"The basketball player?"

"Yes. Isn't that who you were talking about?"

"No. I was referring to her boyfriend from back home, Dan Gentry. She was seeing AJ Harris?"

Rachel shrugged her shoulders. "They were on again-off again. I'm not sure if they were on or off when she died."

"But she was with Bowe the night she died."

"She was," Rachel said with a sigh. "I guess they were off."

Chase shook his head like a dog, trying to clear it. Every time he turned around, something new popped up. "Okay. Let's take a step back. I talked to the old boyfriend, Dan, and he told me he had picked her up from the dorm and returned her. He claims he watched her enter the building. You told me the last you saw of her was when you threw her out of the room earlier in the night. Is that still your story?"

Rachel shook her head. "I swear I didn't see her again. I fell asleep at some point, but if she returned to the room, I would have heard her."

"So the last time she was seen alive was when she entered the dorm… " Chase let the statement hang in the air, as if he expected an answer.

Rachel shrugged again. "I guess so. Maybe she called AJ or went to see him. Have you checked with him?"

Chase smiled a tolerant smile and said, "The first I heard

of AJ was two minutes ago. So, no, I haven't checked with him."

He felt like he was at the grocery store, bouncing back and forth across the store, from aisle to aisle, because he could never find what he was looking for. Only the points of his bouncing were an hour's drive apart.

Could Aley have called AJ Harris after returning to the dorm? Well, of course, she could have; she told Dan Gentry that she had to fix things. Was her relationship with AJ one of the things? Did AJ know that she had been with Bowe that night? Chances were pretty good that he had been at the same party. Could he have been jealous? Jealous enough to kill her?

Chase dug his cell phone out of his pocket and called Mo Warrick. He asked if they had tracked down Aley's cell-phone records. Warrick didn't know but told Chase he'd find out and get back to him.

Andy Clinton was feeling pretty good about his case. He had Bradlee with the girl at the party and following her from the party. He had Bradlee's DNA in the dead girl and enough circumstantial evidence to suggest it wasn't consensual, including a prior allegation of rape. He also had a manual strangulation. The defense would probably put on an expert that would claim anybody was capable of doing the deed; but, come on, would Mrs. Juror with the grip strength of a sparrow believe that she could do it? Hell no. But a big buck nigger from the streets? Absolutely! So yes, he was feeling pretty good about his case. He was just waiting for the call from the DA's office to tell him when he was to appear before the grand jury.

He smiled rather smugly when Commander Warrick appeared at his cubicle.

"Sergeant," Warrick said.

Clinton almost burst out laughing. Warrick hated him but

obviously wanted something from him and was trying not to show his hatred. "What can I do for you, Commander?"

"I'm looking for the cell-phone records from the Aley Beach case."

Cell-phone records? He had those, didn't he? He remembered ordering them from the cell-phone company. What had he done with them? He sifted through the stack of documents in his In-Box. About halfway down, he found a large white envelope with a Verizon logo on it. He pulled it out of the stack and tore it open. A letter on the top page said the records he had requested followed.

"Got them right here," he said, holding them up.

"Great," Warrick said, biting back the condescension he felt. "Can I get a copy?"

Clinton knew that Warrick would turn them over to Chase, but he was feeling so good about his case and the way that Warrick was kowtowing to him that he didn't care. "Sure, Commander. Let me just run down to the copier and make you a copy."

Warrick smiled. It was pained and Clinton loved it. "I'm headed that way," Warrick said. "I'll join you."

The two men walked to the copier. Clinton dropped the pages into the document feeder and pushed the "start" button. Warrick grabbed the copies that spit out and walked away without another word. Clinton watched him and mumbled, "Fuck you, nigger."

Clinton leafed through the pages as he walked back to his cube. There were many pages. It was almost inconceivable that one person could use a phone that much and still participate in life. He reached the last page as he was entering his cube and almost missed his chair as he sat. He looked at the date and time of the last two calls and felt his stomach drop and his mood with it.

He picked up the phone and dialed Northern. "We got a problem."

Chapter 34

Chase had finished the drive into the city—complete with a stop for sixty bucks worth of gas—and had parked Sarge's truck in the lot behind O'Ryan's when Warrick called back.

"I got the cell-phone records from Clinton," Warrick said.

"So Clinton had them this whole time?"

"Yes."

"So there must not be anything on them," Chase said, giving Clinton the benefit of the doubt.

"I don't know," Warrick said. "He hadn't even opened them. I'm looking at them now. What am I looking for?"

"Did she call anyone after 2 a.m or so?"

Warrick hesitated while he scanned the document. "Yes. One call at 2:17 and one at 4:22. The first call is to a 989-area code. Not sure where that is. North of here, I'm sure."

Chase shook his head. Fucking Clinton. He hadn't even opened the records? So much for giving the prick the benefit of the doubt.

"The other call is in the 313-area code. Local."

"The first call is probably her old boyfriend from back home," he told Warrick. "She called him and asked him to come into the city to meet her."

"Did he?"

"Yeah, but he didn't kill her." Chase was sure of that now, unless she had called somebody else after she was dead. "Can you get the owner of the second phone number?" He'd lay ten-to-one odds that it would come back to AJ Harris.

"I'm sure I can, Mr. Chase," Warrick said.

Chase chuckled. "Sorry, Mo. I could probably get it, but I thought I'd give you a chance to flex some of your tremendous muscle."

Warrick laughed. "Uh huh." He stopped talking, and Chase heard the sound of computer keys clicking in a hunt-and-peck pattern. "The number comes back to a Vernon Daniels."

"Really?" Dammit. He was sure it would be Harris. "Who the hell is Vernon Daniels?"

"I don't know," Warrick said. "I've got a meeting I have to get to. Be sure to let me know if you come up with anything."

"Yeah, thanks," Chase said, but Warrick had already hung up.

Vernon Daniels? Who the hell was Vernon Daniels? Chase wanted to pull his hair out, but he had noticed that it had been getting a little thin lately, so he didn't. He called Andy Clinton and bounced around the department's phone tree for a couple of minutes.

"Who's Vernon Daniels?" he said when at last Clinton came on the phone.

"How do you know about Vernon Daniels?"

"I'm a detective dumb-ass. Finding out things is what I do."

"You're not a detective anymore," Clinton hissed.

"Yeah. Thanks for mentioning that to the Beaches."

"They have a right to know that you are not a representative of the Detroit Police Department."

"Okay, whatever," Chase said, exasperated. He regretted calling the jack ass. "Just tell me who Vernon Daniels is.'

"I don't know."

"Bullshit! Aley Beach called him at 4:22 a.m. the night she disappeared, *long* after she had left the party where she was seen with Bowe Bradlee."

Clinton stuck to his guns. "Vernon Daniels is not a subject of the investigation."

A thought crept into Chase's head. "You don't know who

he is, do you?" he said. "This thing is coming apart on you, Andy. Stop being a douche bag and start following the evidence, or I'm going to shove this thing so far up your ass you're going to wish the department would give you the deal they gave me. By the time I'm done with you, you'll be lucky if all that happens is you get fired. I won't rest until you're in prison for obstruction or something."

"Fuck you, Chase!"

"Yeah, fuck me," Chase said, but again he was talking to dead air. Clinton had already hung up.

He stayed where he was in the driver's seat and tried to figure out how to find Vernon Daniels. He flipped open his cell phone and called Rachel Corrigan. It would have been so much more convenient to have called her the last time instead of driving all the way to Port Huron, but Chase hadn't thought to get her phone number the time before when he had talked to her. He had been too busy showing off with Peter Pan quotes.

Rachel answered on the first ring. It was probably the only positive of cell phones never leaving teenagers' hands. "One more question," Chase said.

"Okay," she said, not sounding at all like it was okay.

Chase ignored the tone of her voice. "Have you ever heard of a guy named Vernon Daniels?"

Rachel sighed. "I don't think so."

"This is important, Rachel."

She sighed louder and paused. Chase waited her out. Finally she said, "You know... maybe I have heard that name. Yeah, I remember now. I remember hearing AJ talking about a guy named Vernon Daniels."

"In what way? Is he a teammate? A friend?"

"I really don't remember. Why don't you ask AJ?"

"I will," Chase said. "Do you know where I can find him?"

"Right now? No, I don't know AJ Harris' schedule."

"Where does he live?"

"In the same building as Bowe. I'm not sure what apartment, but I'm sure it's in the same building... on the same floor, in fact."

Chapter 35

Chase didn't even get out of the truck. He fired her back up and headed back to aisle two, the University Towers apartments. He climbed up to Bowe's floor and skipped the knock; nobody answered them anyway. The door was unlocked so he entered the room. Nic Langdon sat in the same spot playing the same video game.

"Hey!" Chase said to get his attention.

Langdon paused the game and looked up, irritated. "Do I know you?" he said with no recognition.

"I was here the other day. I asked you about the party that the girl went missing from."

The kid turned back to his game and un-paused it. "I told you I don't know anything."

"Yeah, I got that part, and I'm beginning to believe that you don't know anything about anything. I'm looking for AJ Harris. What apartment is his?"

Either Langdon wasn't offended by Chase's dig, or he didn't get it. "Two down, toward the stairs," he said.

"Thanks," Chase said. He turned to leave.

"But he ain't there."

Chase stopped and turned back. "Do you know when he'll be back?"

"Won't."

"What do you mean 'won't'? Won't what?"

"Won't be back."

Chase stepped between the kid and the game on the big-screen TV. "What?"

"Man," the kid said, "I'm 'a bust you up side your head you don't get out the way."

Chase remembered Mo Warrick telling him to stop beating up college kids, so he ignored the threat. "Where'd AJ go?"

"He's gone, man. Left school the day after we got knocked out the tournament. 'Gonna turn pro,' he said."

"Shit," Chase said. He slowly walked to the door and then turned back. "You wouldn't happen to know a guy named Vernon Daniels, would you?"

The kid looked at Chase for a split second out of the corner of his eye. "No."

Now why didn't he believe that?

Byron "Stump" Larson sat behind a small metal desk in the bowels of Thunderbird Arena. Thick forearms covered in a tangle of gray hair rested on the desk top, thick fingers laced in a prayerful pose. He wore a black polo shirt with the Thunderbird logo stitched in green on the left breast.

Stump had been the head basketball coach at D State as long as Chase could remember. His success had been up and down over the years. He had won his share of conference championships and had made the NCAA tournament a respectful number of times for a small school and had even managed a couple of good runs in the tournament. This was supposed to have been the team to take him all the way, but a first-round loss had been unexpected and disappointing.

The disappointment radiated from Stump; and, for the first time that Chase could remember, he looked his age.

Chase took a seat in a metal folding chair. "Thanks for seeing me, Coach."

"Yeah," Stump said, his voice ragged from decades of screaming.

"I wanted to talk to you about Bowe Bradlee."

Stump shook his head. "I haven't seen Bowe in a while."

"Nobody has," Chase said. Well, he had, but he wasn't giving that up.

Stump finally looked at Chase. "What do you mean?" He was genuinely concerned.

"He took off. He's been in hiding ever since the police

questioned him about the girl's disappearance."

"What girl?"

Was it possible that the coach really didn't know anything about what was going on? He sure didn't seem to.

"There was a party at Bowe's apartment the night you guys won your conference tournament and qualified for the NCAAs. A girl went missing, and the police questioned Bowe about it. He denied any knowledge but took off and has been in hiding ever since."

Stump looked at Chase like he was an alien with a monkey head. "Bowe would never hurt anybody," he said. "He's a good kid. And besides, he has too much going for him to do something that stupid. He's worked too hard and has too much to lose."

Chase nodded. He agreed with Stump's assessment, except maybe the part about not ever hurting anybody. "He was accused of rape two years ago."

"The girl recanted her story," Stump said in a dismissive voice.

"Why would she do that?"

"How do I know? Why did she say it was rape to begin with?"

"Is there a chance she recanted because someone paid her off?"

Stump's eyes glazed over. "I wouldn't know anything about something like that."

"I'd think you would know *everything* about what goes on with your players," Chase said.

"I coach basketball," Stump said defensively. "We have people who look out for the kids off the court: tutors, managers, whatever."

"What about AJ Harris?"

"What about him?"

"Do you know where he is?"

Stump shook his head slowly. "He quit."

"Quit?"

"He declared for the draft... thinks he's ready."

"You don't agree?"

"He's a sophomore," Stump said. "He played second fiddle to Bowe the last two years. Yes, he put up good numbers, but that was because the other teams were double- and triple-teaming Bowe. Hell, I could have put up the numbers AJ did if nobody covered me either. Without Bowe to draw the defense, the kid won't stand a chance. He doesn't have the ability to get his own shot."

"So maybe this is the best time for him to leave," Chase countered. "With Bowe gone, his weaknesses will be exposed; maybe now is the time for him to go and get what he can get."

Stump nodded. "Maybe you're right. I guess I didn't look at it that way. I just see a kid who's not ready."

"So you don't know where he is?"

Stump shook his head. "I imagine he's off somewhere getting ready for the draft."

"Okay," Chase said. "One more question, if you don't mind."

"Shoot."

"You ever heard of a guy named Vernon Daniels?"

Daggers shot from Stump's eyes. Through gritted teeth, he said, "That man has nothing to do with my program."

Chase almost laughed at the visceral reaction. "So you have heard of him?"

"He's one of those... those... hangers-on or whatever you call them. Likes to hang around the kids and feel important, like he's part of the team or something."

"Like a booster?"

"He's not a booster," Stump hissed. "He has absolutely no standing with my program. He does not recruit for my program, and he does not speak for my program. Understood?"

"Got it," Chase said. He had a pretty good idea where Vernon Daniels came in.

Chapter 36

When Chase was a kid, his parents would take him to his uncle's farm outside of the city every summer for a family reunion. There was a small pond on the farm that nobody ever swam in because it was full of leeches. A bunch of blood-sucking leeches that nobody wanted anything to do with. In the world of Detroit school-boy basketball, the pond the leeches hung out in was the AAU circuit.

The Amateur Athletic Union was an outstanding program that gave kids a chance to compete and develop skills. Like most good things, it had been ruined by selfish people with bad intentions. Chase was pretty sure that Vernon Daniels was one of the selfish people who ruined good things and that that was where he fit into the story.

For whatever reason, these guys befriend the kids and their families. They give them money and presents to embed themselves with the family. They then try to influence the kids to go to the high school and college they want them to attend, thus ingraining themselves with the high school and college program... all in an attempt to feel important, like a big shot. Of course, this is against NCAA rules; and most coaches don't want anything to do with these guys, which explained Stump Larson's reaction when Chase had asked if he knew Vernon Daniels.

Chase didn't know anything about the AAU circuit's schedule, so he called the one person he thought would know, Ty Jackson. Ty didn't know the schedule either because recruiting is against the rules in Detroit high school basketball; of course, that didn't stop many of the coaches from doing it, but it did stop Ty. He was a rule-follower, which was one of the reasons Chase thought so highly of him. Since there would be no reason for a coach to attend an

AAU tournament, other than to recruit the kids to his school, Ty had no reason to know the schedule. He had, however, heard of Vernon Daniels and many others like him; and they all made him sick, so he readily agreed to help Chase track him down.

The two men entered a fifty-year-old high school gym downriver from Detroit. It was warm and reeked of decades of stale sweat, just like every other gym in every other high school in America. Shoes squeaked on the wood floor, and the ball pounded over and over. Coaches yelled encouragement from the sidelines, and parents yelled instructions from the stands. It should have been the other way around, but it never was.

Ty spotted Daniels immediately and pointed him out to Chase. His light-brown skin was tinged slightly yellow. He sat four rows up from center court, wearing a black and green wannabe D State tracksuit with a thick gold chain and the latest LeBron shoes. His foot was on the bleacher in front of him and his right wrist rested on his knee, giving all around a good look at the ring on his hand. It looked like a championship ring of some sort. Probably college. Probably bought on eBay.

Chase climbed to the fifth row and sat just to the left of his shoulder. Ty stayed by the entrance. He didn't want to be anywhere near Daniels. Chase rested his foot on the bleacher in front of him, right next to Daniels. Daniels registered the foot and looked briefly at the man it belonged to and then back to the court.

"Any talent out there?" Chase said.

Daniels pointed at the ten-year-old handling the ball. "Point guard on the team in white. Moves like a water bug and has the ball on a string."

Chase watched. The kid bounced the ball at the top of the key while he surveyed the court. Without warning, he exploded into action, crossing over the kid guarding him and blasting down the lane. The defender fell to the floor trying to react to the lightening-quick movement, and the kid with the ball was laying it off the backboard and through the hoop before anyone else on the defense could react.

Daniels laughed and raised his hand for a high-five. Chase left him hanging.

"You Vernon Daniels?"

Daniels stopped laughing and let his hand fall back to his knee. "That's right. Who's asking?"

"I wanted to ask you about a phone call you received."

"I said, 'who's asking?'" Daniels said.

"Turns out you were the last person the girl called before she was murdered."

"Wait. What?"

"Aley Beach," Chase said. "The girl who was murdered up at D State." He pointed to the logo on Daniels' chest. "You can't have missed it; it's been on TV pretty much non-stop. She called you before she was murdered."

"You must be mistaken, my man. I didn't talk to no murdered girl."

"I'd like to believe you, Vern, but phone records don't lie."

Daniels shook his head emphatically. "I never talked to that girl."

"Come on, Vern," Chase said. "Who do you think the jury will believe? You or the phone company?"

"Listen," Daniels said. "I don't even know who you are, but I have one of those plans where I have ten phones on my plan. She could have called any one of them. But she did not call me."

Chase cocked his head to the side. "Now why would you have ten cell phones on your plan, Vern?"

Daniels looked around nervously. "I... uh... you know, pass them around to some of the kids. Help them out when their parents can't."

Chase shook his head disgustedly. A cascade of oohs and ahs and laughs filled the gym. Chase looked to the court to see the white team's point guard jogging back down the court, high-fiving his teammates, and the poor kid guarding him picking himself up off the court again.

He turned his attention back to the leech. "Does AJ Harris have one of those phones?"

Daniels sighed. "Yes."

Apparently the "help" didn't comprise taking the fall for murder.

"So the girl called AJ. Did he then call you?"

"What?"

"You know... 'Hey, Vern, I got a problem.'"

"No! Absolutely not!"

"Why don't I believe that?"

"Why would I kill some girl I don't even know?"

"I don't know," Chase said. "Why are you here watching a bunch of ten-year-olds? Why do you give them money and cars... and cell phones?"

"Come on, man," Daniels said. "I'm just trying to help these kids out. Some of them will never get the chance to succeed without guys like me."

Chase snorted a laugh. "You're a piece of work, Vern," he said. "So where's AJ?"

AJ Harris sprinted from the corner of the court along the baseline under the hoop to the other corner of the court. In one motion, he spun back to the basket, caught a pass from a kid at the top of the key and fired a jump shot. *Swish!* Before the ball had cleared the net, he was sprinting the baseline back to the corner where he had started. He spun, caught the pass and fired up another shot. *Swish!*

Chase watched from the bleachers as Harris repeated the procedure at least ten times, making a little more than half of the shots. They were in a gym that reminded Chase of the gym from the movie *Hoosiers*. He hated to admit it, but he went to fifth and sixth grade in a school just like it, with the same gym. How did he get so damn old?

The scene playing out before him was a microcosm of the fairness of life. AJ was working his ass off while Bowe was living it up in a swanky hotel, drinking champagne and maybe snorting coke with hookers. Chase didn't know for sure that he had been the one doing the coke; it could have been the girl's. Bowe was probably going to be the first pick in the draft, and AJ would be lucky to be drafted at all.

At one point a shot went long and caromed off the rim, bouncing toward the bleachers. Chase retrieved it but held onto it rather than throw it back into the rotation. There was a kid under the basket rebounding and one at the top of the key feeding passes to AJ. They had a good rhythm going with two balls. Chase holding one of them threw off that rhythm. They franticly tried to keep AJ supplied, but eventually AJ turned and there was no ball there.

"Ball!" he yelled.

The kid rebounding had chased a missed shot into the corner and struggled to corral it.

"Ball!" AJ yelled again.

Chase dribbled his ball and walked casually onto the court.

AJ saw him. "You're fucking up my workout, old man."

Old man?

"I need to talk to you," Chase said.

"I know you?"

"Probably not."

"Then get the fuck outta here and let me work."

Chase did not get the fuck outta there. "I need to talk to you about your girlfriend."

"I ain't got no girlfriend," AJ said.

"Well, not any more. She's dead."

AJ studied Chase for a moment. He wasn't as tall as

Bowe or Nic Langdon, but he still had Chase by four or five inches. Sweat rolled off his bald head like rain off a fresh wax job. Without looking at him, AJ told the kid feeding his passes to take a break. "Go get some water or something."

The passer and the rebounder both left the gym. Chase passed the ball he held to AJ. He shot automatically. *Swish!*

"She called you," Chase said, "the night she disappeared."

"So what if she did? Don't mean I killed her. Besides, I was sleeping. The call went to voicemail."

"What'd she say?"

"I don't know. Just some bullshit about she loved me and she was sorry 'bout everything."

"Things weren't going well between you two?"

"I ain't got time for alla that, ya know?" He held out his arms. "This is all I got time for right now. I ain't Bowe. I got one shot to make it in the league. I fuck this up and I'll be eating fuckin' Spaghettios, playing in Italy. There be time for alla that other shit later."

Chase had to give it to the kid; he had his priorities straight. But where did that leave a love-struck teenage girl?

"Did she say anything else in the message?"

"Said she needed a place to crash."

"Did you let her crash at your place?"

"I tol' you, I was already asleep. I didn't get the message until the next day."

And she was already gone by then.

"Can I get back to work now?" AJ said.

"Sure." Chase picked up the ball where it had come to rest and passed it back to AJ. He heard it *swish* through the net as he left the gym.

Chapter 37

Mo Warrick was deep in thought, sitting on a bench on the Riverwalk, staring across the Detroit River at Windsor, Ontario. He wore a black wool overcoat over a gray suit with a pink tie. He looked like a stockbroker or a lawyer, definitely not a cop. He munched absently on a hotdog while he thought whatever deep thought he was thinking. Chase sat on the bench next to him.

"You remember the hotdogs at Tiger Stadium?" Warrick said, not looking at him.

"Sure."

"Those were damn good hotdogs. I've often wondered if it was the hotdog that was so good, or if the atmosphere had something to do with it."

That's what he had been deep in thought about? Hotdogs? "They were good," Chase agreed. "Of course, I was just a kid. The excitement of being at Tiger Stadium and all, they probably could've given me shit on a stick, and it would have tasted good."

Warrick nodded and finished off the hotdog. "They're going to indict Bowe tomorrow," he said, balling up the hotdog wrapper.

"Shit."

"Yep."

"He didn't do it, Mo."

"Apparently, that doesn't matter. They have enough to indict. She was seen with him, and there is evidence of sexual assault."

"Tommy Chin will testify that that evidence could have been from consensual sex with a well-endowed man."

"I doubt they'll ask him that in front of the grand jury."

Fucking Andy Clinton. "Can't you stop it?"

"Did it stop you when an assistant chief told you to stop?"

"No, but…. Shit, Mo, why is Clinton pushing this?"

"Probably because he's a racist motherfucker, and he can't stand to see a young black man cash in on more money than his worthless white ass could ever dream of making. He's jealous, and this is his chance to take the kid down and feel better about himself. Plus, he wants to stick it to you the same way you stuck it to his wife."

"He needs to get over that," Chase said. "What about the DA? She's black."

An ironic smile creased Mo's face. "I don't know," he said. "Maybe she wants to be mayor."

Chase sighed.

Warrick stood and brushed off the front of his coat. "We've got until tomorrow morning to solve this thing."

Chase continued to sit and look at Canada while Warrick walked away. What happened after Aley Beach reentered the dorm? For all he knew, Bowe could have gone back and killed her later to cover up the rape. Or AJ could have done it because he found out she had slept with Bowe. Or Rachel Corrigan could have done it in a jealous fit. Or Howard Frazier could have had Kendrick Martin do it to protect his investment. Or Vernon Daniels could have done it to try and curry favor with Bowe. Or. Or. Or. Just because she was back in the dorm didn't guarantee that she stayed there. She could have left the dorm again and gotten strangled by a stranger.

He pushed up from the bench and headed back to Sarge's truck, which he had borrowed again. His route was blocked by the now-familiar black Escalade owned by Howard Frazier. Kendrick Martin stood next to the driver's door.

"Not today, Kendrick," Chase said. "I'm not in the mood."

"I don't give a fuck what your mood is," the big man

said. "Mr. Frazier wants to talk to you."

"I'm busy."

Kendrick assumed his Superman stance—feet spread with hands on hips, pulling open his black leather coat to reveal the gun he carried.

Chase walked up to him and, without missing stride, kicked him between the legs. Kendrick bent at the waist and put his hands on his knees, gasping for air, but he didn't fall. He was one tough son of a bitch. Chase had gotten all his stuff with that kick.

He double-timed it around the Escalade before Kendrick regained his breath. He had just reached the truck when he heard Frazier yell at him.

"Chase!"

Chase turned around and faced the SUV. The passenger-side rear window was down, and Frazier's face filled the opening.

"They're going to the grand jury tomorrow," Frazier said.

"I know. I'm working on it."

"Well, work faster!"

Chapter 38

Dennis Harden sat sideways behind his small desk. His tailbone must have been perched on the edge of the seat because his shoulder barely cleared the desktop. He wore the mint-green uniform shirt, short-sleeved. An outstretched beefy forearm lay flat on the desktop. He drummed his fingers and looked at Chase.

"If I give you this information and you're wrong, we'll both be in a world of shit."

"Well, you will be," Chase said and smiled.

Harden didn't return the smile.

Chase turned serious. He had walked the campus police chief through every step of Aley Beach's last night, from the party to exiting Dan Gentry's truck and reentering the dorm. "I'm not wrong, Dennis. Somebody in that dorm did this; it's the only logical conclusion. And chances are very good that he had been in trouble before."

"I get fired and my wife is going to kill me," Harden said.

Chase chuckled. "You've still got your pension from the DPD."

"It's not the money. She can't deal with me being home all the time. This job keeps me out of the house."

"You lost the bet, Dennis," Chase said.

Harden thought a little more and then sighed. "I know I'm going to regret this," he said.

He sat up straight and turned to the computer on the corner of the desk. He grabbed the mouse and clicked something and typed something, then clicked and typed again and then squinted at the screen. "So what? Am I supposed to go to the bathroom or something while you look at the screen even though I tell you not to?"

Chase shrugged. "If you want."

Harden didn't leave. He waved Chase to his side of the desk. Chase rounded the desk and looked at the screen over Harden's shoulder. A complete list of every complaint lodged against anybody living in the dorm in the last two years was displayed in green letters against a black background. One name jumped off the screen as if in 3D.

"Well, son of a bitch," Chase said. He pointed at the name on the screen. "What'd that kid do?"

Harden pointed the mouse and clicked and typed, then clicked and typed again. Another screen with neon-green letters appeared.

"Let's see," Harden said. "Looks like a complaint was filed by a young lady who was receiving a little more attention from the young man than she wanted. Text messages, emails, unwanted advances. Apparently, he tried to kiss her one night when she had had a little too much to drink. That's what triggered the complaint."

"What happened?"

"One of my officers paid him a visit and told him to knock it off."

"And that was it?"

"I guess so. There is nothing else in the file."

"So he just stopped?"

"I guess so, Chase," Harden said. "What do you want me to say? There's nothing else here."

"Okay. Okay," Chase said. "Don't have a cow."

Harden sat back from the computer, reclining his chair. "You going to talk to the kid?"

"Absolutely."

Harden took a breath and let it out through his nose. "Okay. Let me send one of my officers with you."

"I don't need a babysitter, Dennis," Chase said.

"Yes, you do," Harden replied.

The officer assigned to babysitting duty was named Boyd. He was in his early thirties, just over six feet and in good shape. Why would this guy be working for a campus police force instead of a city? He seemed a perfect candidate for the street. But maybe he was too smart for that. Why go out there and risk getting shot when he can spend his days rousting frat boys? Not everybody needed gangbangers shooting at him to feel alive, like Chase did. Boyd wore the same two-tone green uniform as Harden, along with a wide leather gun belt, complete with gun, handcuffs and taser.

They met at the dorm entrance and entered together. Chase wasn't sure if Boyd had been briefed on what they were doing there, so he asked.

"Just going to talk to the kid, right?" he said.

"Right," Chase said, "but be ready for anything. I'm not sure how this is going to go."

Chase really didn't know how it was going to go. What would he find behind the dorm-room door? A barricaded gunman? Probably not. But his years of experience taught him that it was the most unexpected suspects that surprised you the most, so he kept his shit wired.

Chase knocked on the door and a voice said to come in. He motioned Boyd to the side of the door opening. Chase stood clear of the opening on the other side. He turned the doorknob and pushed, hoping all hell didn't break loose.

Todd, the resident advisor, sat on a twin bed pushed into the corner of the small room. He leaned against the wall at the head of the bed, legs crossed at the ankles. He held a book in his hands, his right index finger sandwiched between the pages holding his place.

Chase entered first. Boyd followed.

"Hi, guys," Todd said. "What's up?" He acted as if cops showing up at his door was common.

"We need to have a few words," Boyd said.

"Sure. About what?"

"Aley Beach," Chase said.

Todd's face clouded over. "Oh. I don't really know anything, but I guess I can try to help."

Boyd must have felt the same negative vibe that Chase did. His right hand moved slightly. It hovered near the taser, not the gun. "Why don't you put the book down, Todd?" he said.

Todd dog-eared the page and set the book on the bed next to him. He held his hands up in mock surrender, a smile creasing his face. "What's going on?"

Chase grabbed the desk chair from its place in the knee hole and set it next to the bed. He sat backward on it, forearms crossed on the backrest. His face was very near to Todd's. "Where were you the night Aley disappeared?"

Todd's hands dropped to his lap. "What? I was right here."

"Was anyone with you?"

"No. I was alone. Why?"

"Did you happen to see her that night? Aley?"

"No."

"You know what I think, Boyd," Chase said, keeping his eyes on Todd. "I think Todd here heard Aley come in and heard her phone call to AJ Harris. He heard her tell him she needed a place to sleep and figured it was finally his chance. She had nowhere else to go."

"No," Todd said, shaking his head. "I didn't see or hear anything."

He was lying. Chase had been lied to by the best, and this kid was nowhere near the best.

"Then what happened?" Boyd asked Chase, playing along.

"She rejected him," Chase said.

Todd shook his head.

Chase ignored him and spoke to Boyd. "She had nowhere else to go, and she still rejected him. She'd have rather slept outside in the cold than in his bed."

"That's cold, man," Boyd said.

"No," Todd said.

"So he got angry," Chase continued. "He grabbed her and dragged her in here."

"No," Todd said again.

"Yes," Chase said, nodding. "That's exactly what happened."

"So why'd he kill her?" Boyd said.

"I didn't."

"She laughed at him," Chase said.

Todd shook his head, but his face had flushed.

"Aley Beach was at the lowest point of her life—rejected by the man she loved, with nowhere to go, but Todd still wasn't good enough for her. She laughed at you, didn't she, Todd? She laughed at you for thinking you were."

Todd stopped shaking his head and gritted his teeth. "Bitch," he said.

"Yeah, bitch," Chase said. "Who did she think she was? Some farm girl from the sticks? And she thinks she's better than you?"

"Stuck-up bitch," Todd said. "She'll spread her legs for those... basketball players, but not me?"

Chase nodded. "You snapped. I don't blame you. I would have too. Bitch like that thinks she's too good for me. After all I tried to do for her?"

Todd was nodding now. "I did try," he said.

"So you killed her."

Todd was still nodding, but Chase wanted him to say it. "Tell me what happened, Todd. Did you kiss her?"

"She pushed me away."

"And that angered you. So you hit her."

Tears started to form in his eyes. "I didn't mean to, but I was so mad."

"I understand. I would have too. So then what?"

"She tried to hit me back, but I blocked it."

"And then you grabbed her throat."

Tears flowed freely down Todd's face. He nodded. "I grabbed her throat."

"And you squeezed."

Todd nodded.

"Say it, Todd," Chase said.

"I squeezed," he said.

"You squeezed until she was dead."

"Yes."

Chapter 39

Laura Phillips filled the screen of the TV mounted in the corner above the bar. Her blonde hair and makeup were both perfect. She beamed behind a serious expression as she reported on the murder of Aley Beach to a national audience. Chase had asked her to leave him out of it, which she graciously did, giving the credit for the arrest to Officer Boyd of the Detroit State University Police. She had parlayed the story into a slot with the national show, finally getting her break.

Chase was happy for her, as well as for Bowe Bradlee, who, with the confession and arrest of Todd the RA, was no longer a suspect in the murder. He was once again being projected as the number-one pick in the upcoming draft. Rumor had it that the Pistons were pulling out all the stops to get that pick. Chase hoped they failed. He loved his hometown team, but the kid needed to get as far away from Detroit as possible. Sacramento or Portland would be good.

The outside door opened, and Wanda Jackson entered O'Ryan's. Chase smiled, but the smile wasn't returned. He really hoped he wasn't the one who was putting that look on her face.

"Hi, Wanda," he said. "Buy you a drink?"

"No." Her lips were pressed together and arms folded across her chest.

Chase waited for her to say something. She didn't.

"What's up, Wanda?"

Wanda looked down at her feet for a beat and then back at Chase. "I want you to take me to Bowe."

"Why?"

"I'm worried about him."

"He's fine."

"I need to see that for myself."

"Does Ty know you're here?" Chase said and immediately knew it had been a mistake.

Now he *was* definitely the one who was putting that look on her face. "I don't need Ty's permission," she snapped.

"Of course not," Chase said, trying to recover. "It's just…"

"Just what?"

Chase sighed, defeated. "Nothing. Can you drive? My car isn't up for the trip."

"What's wrong with your car?"

"It's got a couple of holes in the engine block."

Wanda looked as if she wanted to ask for more details but decided against it. "Come on."

Chase climbed into the passenger seat of a brilliant white Chevy Cobalt and felt the roof looming just over his head. He resisted the urge to duck by scooting his ass forward, which lowered his head but crammed his knees against the dashboard. It was going to be a long ride to Birmingham.

"So what has you worried?" he said to break the tense silence that filled the small car.

Wanda gripped the steering wheel and stared at the road. "His phone is going straight to voicemail, and he's not responding to my texts."

"Probably dead."

Her head snapped in Chase's direction, and the car swerved violently. "Why would you say that?"

Chase grabbed the oh-shit handle above the window and prepared for a collision. Wanda yanked the car back into the correct lane.

Chase was baffled and then realized she thought he meant Bowe was probably dead. "The phone," he said. "The phone is probably dead."

Wanda breathed a sigh of relief. She was wound a little tighter than Chase had thought.

"Why would you jump to the conclusion that I was saying Bowe was probably dead?"

"I don't know. I'm just worried about that boy. He *is* still a boy, you know. He might be built like a man, but he's only nineteen years old."

"I know," Chase said, "but it's over. They have the killer in custody. Bowe is in the clear."

"Then why isn't he answering his phone?"

Chase didn't venture another guess after the way his last one had gone. He told her he didn't know, and they rode the rest of the way in silence.

Wanda said, "Well, will you look at this place," as they pulled to a stop in front of the Townsend Hotel. "Where does a college kid get the money for a place like this?"

"His agent is paying for it."

"Probably not out of the goodness of his heart."

"Probably not," Chase agreed. "I'm sure he's expecting some sort of recompense when Bowe signs his first contract."

Wanda shook her head. "Shameful that a grown man would take advantage of a kid like that."

"I agree."

"I just wish Ty or I had known and been able to protect Bowe."

Chase didn't know what to say, so he didn't say anything at all.

They climbed from the car (it was much easier for Wanda than for Chase) and entered the hotel. Chase led the way to the elevator, and they rode to Bowe's floor in silence. Wanda fidgeted in the hallway when their knock went unanswered. Chase knocked again. Same result.

"Something's wrong," Wanda said.

"Don't jump to conclusions," Chase said. "Let's go find somebody who can let us in."

Chase took Wanda's arm and guided her to the elevator. In

the lobby they approached the front desk and asked the perky young lady behind the counter if Bowe had checked out. She tapped at her computer and shook her head, no record of him checking out.

"Something's wrong," Wanda said again.

Chase walked to the front door to the young bell hop, waiting for new guests with bags to carry.

"Do you know who Bowe Bradlee is?" he asked the young man.

"Of course," the kid said as if Chase were an idiot to even ask.

Chase brushed it off. It wasn't the first time he had had the tone directed at him. Probably wouldn't be the last. "Have you seen him today?"

"I'm not sure." It was the I-need-a-tip-before-answering stall.

"Young man," Wanda cut in, "we don't have time to play games here. If you saw him, you had better tell us."

The kid looked at Chase.

"I wouldn't mess with her if I were you," Chase said.

"Yeah, okay," the kid said. "I saw him a couple of hours ago getting into a car with some other guys."

"Was he okay?" Wanda asked.

The kid shrugged. "He seemed to be."

"Describe the car and the guys," Chase said.

The kid shrugged again. He was good at it. "Black guys. Lots of tats. Gangbangers like."

"Shit," Chase said. "What about the car?"

The kid went with his go-to shrug. "I don't know. It was like a four-door sedan. Older. Beat to hell."

Chase thanked the kid and slipped him a five-dollar bill. He then turned to Wanda.

"Atari?" she said.

"Be my guess."

"You think Atari would hurt him?"

211

"I don't think so," Chase said. "My guess is he's using Bowe as bait."

"Bait for what?"

"Me."

Chapter 40

Wanda and Chase fought about how to handle the situation all the way back to Detroit. Chase finally got her to agree to let him handle it. She dropped Chase in front of O'Ryan's and drove off. He wasn't all that sure that she would actually go home and let him handle Atari Black.

Sarge stood behind the bar. He looked up when Chase entered.

"I have a message for you," he said.

"Who from?"

"Some kid, probably nine or ten years old."

"What'd he say?"

"He said, 'If you want him, come get him.'"

Chase laughed. "He sent a kid to deliver his message? Chicken shit."

"Who?"

"Atari Black."

"What's going on?" Sarge said.

Sally had come out from the back room. "Yeah, what's going on, Chase?" she said.

"Bowe Bradlee has disappeared again," Chase said. "It sounds like Atari Black has him this time."

"That's the 'him' in the message," Sarge said.

"Yep."

"You don't think Atari would hurt him, do you?" Sally said.

Chase shook his head. "I don't think so."

"But you can't be sure?"

"No, I can't be sure and I sort of have to do this."

"Sort of have to do what?" Sally said.

"Go get Bowe."

"Why?"

213

"I hit Atari."

"So what? You have to give him a chance to hit you back?"

"If I don't, this will never be over. He'll keep coming after me until the one time when my guard is down and he kills me."

Sally was outraged. "That's the biggest load of horse shit I've ever heard," she said.

"He's right," Sarge said. "He has to put an end to this."

Sally looked at Sarge and back at Chase. The fear was in her eyes again. Chase wanted nothing more than to take her in his arms and run off someplace where she would feel safe. "What's wrong with you two?" she said. "That kid wants to kill you. And you're just going to walk right into his trap?"

"I'm not just going to walk into his trap," Chase said. "My mama raised a fool, but it was my brother."

If life were a crime novel, that was the point where a storm would have blown in. The sky would have darkened, and big fat rain drops would have started to plunk onto the windshield. By the time the confrontation happened, it would be raining so hard that Atari and Chase would have had trouble seeing each other. But in reality, it was the nicest day of the year so far. The sun shone brightly, and the sky was a brilliant blue. The temperature hovered near sixty.

Chase had lied to Sally. He did intend to walk right into Atari's trap.

He parked Sarge's truck at the curb exactly where he had parked the last time he had visited Atari at Brewster-Douglass. He climbed out of the truck with his shotgun in his hand and his Beretta on his hip. As Yogi Berra said, "It was like déjà vu all over again." Only this time, he was alone.

Chase walked across the expanse and onto the basketball court. He felt like Wyatt Earp entering the OK Corral. He held his arms out and yelled, "Here I am! Come out, come out wherever you are, you chicken shit motherfucker!"

He stood there for what seemed like forever, waiting for Atari to appear or shoot him. Sweat streamed down his back. His heart raced to the point of explosion. He took several deep breaths in through his nose and tried not to appear as tense as he actually was. He loosened his grip on the shotgun; it wouldn't do to have his fingers cramp up at the time that he needed them to work.

"Stop being a bitch! Come out here and face me!" he hollered, just begging for a bullet in the head.

A bullet struck a fraction of a second before the report of the shot rang out. Chips of asphalt flew up about ten feet away from Chase. A second shot rang out. The second shot came from behind Chase. And then all hell broke loose.

Chase had called Warrick and updated him on the situation before leaving O'Ryan's. Warrick had insisted on sending a SWAT team. They seemed to have arrived.

The courtyard of the Brewster-Douglass housing project turned into a real-life war movie. Automatic fire rattled from the windows of the crumbling buildings. The SWAT team returned fire from where they had dispersed around the perimeter. And Chase was the fool standing in the crossfire.

He ducked his head and ran for the nearest cover. It just happened to be the wall of one of the abandoned apartment towers occupied by the BD Boyz. He found a stairwell and headed up two steps at a time, still clutching the shotgun in both hands. He had no idea where he was going.

The third-floor landing was guarded by a kid with an automatic pistol held at his side. He couldn't have been more than seventeen or eighteen. His face was as smooth as the proverbial baby's butt. His eyes were glassy and his pupils were pinpoints. He was high on something. Chase stopped a couple of steps short and brought the shotgun around to a firing position.

"Put the gun down!" Chase said. He had to shout to be heard over the war that was playing out in the courtyard. The kid just looked at him. "Come on, kid. Don't make me shoot you."

The kid raised the barrel of his gun, and Chase squeezed his trigger. The blast was deafening in the stairwell. The shot caught the kid up under the ribcage and blew him off his feet and into the wall freshly-painted with the kid's blood. He fell in a heap. His skinny chest looked like raw hamburger.

"Shit!" Chase said.

It was decision time. Had the kid been positioned there for a reason? Obviously. But was the reason to keep anyone from going further up or to keep anyone from entering the floor? Since he hadn't been *in* the stairwell, Chase figured he had been put there to keep anyone from entering the third floor. Of course, as stoned as the kid had been, who knows what he was *supposed* to have been doing?

Chase entered the corridor and picked his way through years of garbage that lined the walls. He peeked into every open apartment, which was all of them since all the doors had been removed. The fourth apartment on the left contained a gunman. His back was to Chase as he fired an automatic rifle out the open window. Chase entered behind him and crept up to within a couple of feet when the gangbanger turned his head. He saw Chase and brought the rifle around. Chase fired, blowing the kid out the window.

He searched the apartment for Bowe. No luck. That would have been too easy anyway.

Further down the corridor, Chase found another kid. He was about twelve. He sat with his back to the wall, knees pulled up to his chest. He rocked from his butt and heels, with his arms circling his knees. He was crying. "Stay down and you'll be all right," Chase said. The crying boy reached a hand for Chase, but he didn't have time to babysit, so he left him there. Later he would wonder if he felt worse about the kids he had killed or the one he had abandoned.

The rest of the floor was empty. Chase double-timed it up

two more flights where he found another teenager with an automatic weapon. This one dropped his weapon when told to do so. "Where's Bowe?" Chase said. The kid pointed down the corridor. "Atari?" The kid nodded and then ran into the stairwell. Chase reloaded and then followed the barrel of his shotgun down the hall.

He looked left and right into the first two open apartments and then stepped past the doorways. He headed for the next set of doors, but an arm snaked around his throat from behind and the barrel of a pistol pressed into the side of his head.

"Now who's the bitch?" Atari mumbled in Chase's ear. "Drop the burner."

Chase couldn't help himself. "I didn't understand you. Got a toothache or something?"

Of course, it was a dumb thing to say. Atari pistol whipped him across the back of the head.

"Ow! Shit!" Chase said and let the shotgun drop to the floor.

Before Atari could do anything further, both men were lifted off the floor. "Let him go, Atari." It was Bowe. He had Atari in a headlock while Atari had Chase in a headlock. It was like a Three Stooges movie. Bowe shook his brother, trying to break his grip. "Let him go."

Atari's grip finally gave, and Chase slipped to the floor.

"You trippin', Bowe?!" Atari yelled.

"This man helped me," Bowe said.

"Fuck that! This cracker suckered me and broke my fuckin face," Atari said. "Nobody do that to Atari Black. He gotta die, Bowe. That why we got him here."

Bowe shook his head. "I was wrong. I shouldn't have helped you set him up. He's a good man. He helped me."

Bowe stepped around his brother, which wasn't easy since he was just about as wide as the corridor, and reached a hand down to Chase. Atari stuck his gun in Bowe's ear.

"This can't go down like this, Bowe," he said. "I can't let this man disrespect me in front of my crew and get away with it."

Bowe didn't flinch. Somewhere inside of him he must have felt that his brother wouldn't kill him. From the crazed look in Atari's eyes, Chase wasn't as sure.

He pulled the Beretta off his hip and pointed it at Atari "Put the gun down, Atari."

Atari looked at Chase and saw the gun pointed at his face. The conflict he felt was evident on his face. He didn't want to shoot Bowe, but he couldn't bring himself to lose to Chase... again.

"What are you going to do?" Chase said. "Kill your brother just to spite me?"

Atari thought for a few more seconds and then said, "Shit!" and took the gun out of Bowe's ear. He then pointed it at Chase. They stared each other down over the pistol sights. "You ready to die for this?" he said.

Bowe reached out and engulfed Atari's hand and gun in his massive grip. "No," he said. "Nobody dies today."

Atari looked up at his brother. Chase almost felt sorry for him. It was clear that he loved his brother and wanted to do right by him, but he couldn't let Chase win. Bowe nodded at Atari, and he finally dropped his hand to his side.

Chase took a deep breath, let it out and lowered his gun.

Atari took a step towards him. "One more thing," he said, then busted Chase in the jaw with the gun in his hand.

The force of the blow bounced Chase's head off the wall and loosened a couple of teeth. He did not retaliate. He had had it coming and wasn't about to escalate a war with the most notorious gangbanger in Detroit.

"Dammit, Atari!" Bowe shouted.

"A'right. A'right," Atari said. "I'm done now."

Chapter 41

Two months later Bowe was drafted by the Minnesota Timberwolves with the first pick in the NBA draft. Chase watched it on the TV above the bar at O'Ryan's. Ty and Wanda Jackson were there with him, as was his agent, Howard Frazier.

The usual drunks and a few other guys were in O'Ryan's. Sally wasn't there. She was taking some time off. She wouldn't tell Chase or Sarge where she was or when she was coming back. Chase missed her.

On the TV Bowe walked up onto the stage and did the whole thing where he put on the team hat and shook hands with the commissioner and got his picture taken. He then exited stage left and was met by the beautiful television reporter, there to interview all the draft picks. Laura Phillips beamed up at him. "Congratulations, Bowe," she said. "How's it feel to be the first pick?"

"Hey, Denzel," one of the usual drunks yelled, "get us another round."

Epilogue

The firefight between the BD Boyz and the Detroit Police was the fuel that motivated the city to finally complete the demolition of the remaining towers of the Brewster-Douglass Housing Project. The blight on the city was finally gone, but memories of better days remained. The marker erected on the spot said in part: "Former residents described Brewster as a 'community filled with families that displayed love, respect and concern for everyone in a beautiful, clean and secure neighborhood.'"

www.ingramcontent.com/pod-product-compliance
Lightning Source LLC
Chambersburg PA
CBHW060431180626
46817CB00007B/2755